FEEDING THE GHOSTS

Fred D'Aguiar

GRANTA

Granta Publications, 12 Addison Avenue, London W11 4QR

Published in Great Britain by Granta Books, 2014
First published in Great Britain by Chatto & Windus Ltd, 1997
Published by Vintage 1998

A CIP catalogue record for this book is available from the British Library.

1 3 5 7 9 10 8 6 4 2

ISBN 978 1 84708 864 2
eISBN 978 1 84708 865 9

Printed and bound by CPI Group (UK) Ltd, Croydon, CR0 4YY

www.grantabooks.com

MIX
Paper from
responsible sources
FSC® C020471

Acknowledgements

I am grateful for the welcomed help and advice from all quarters: Garry Morris and the Trans-Atlantic Slave Gallery on Merseyside; the Black History Resource Group publication, 'Slavery: An Introduction to the African Holocaust' (Liverpool Education Directorate, February 1995); Nigel Rigby at the National Maritime Museum; Graeme Rigby at 'Victoria House'; Sara Holloway; my agent, Bruce Hunter at David Higham Associates; and, especially, Jonathan Burnham and Debbie Dalton.

For Debbie Dalton,
Cameron, Elliot
and to Jonathan Burnham

Where are your monuments, your battles, martyrs?
Where is your tribal memory? Sirs,
in that grey vault. The sea. The sea
has locked them up. The sea is history.

from 'The Sea is History' by Derek Walcott

The stone had skidded arc'd and bloomed into islands

from 'Calypso' by Kamau Brathwaite

Prologue

THE SEA IS slavery. Sea water boils in its own current. Salt gives the sea the texture of fabric, something thick and close-knitted, not unlike the fine dust of a barn seen floating in a shaft of light. Sea receives a body as if that body has come to rest on a cushion, one that gives way to the body's weight and folds around it like an envelope. Over three days 131 such bodies, no, 132, are flung at this sea. Each lands with a sound that the sea absorbs and silences. Each opens a wound in this sea that heals over each body without the evidence of a scar. Two hundred and sixty-four arms and 264 legs punch and kick against a tide that insists all who land on it, all who break its smooth surface, must succumb to its swells, tumbles, pushes and pulls.

Water replaces air in 131 of these bodies. They fight then become still as if changing from struggle to an embrace, seeing in an enemy someone to love and therefore to hold, no longer against water but a part of its thrust from one point of the compass to another. Salt washes wounds on those bodies instilled by the locks, chains, masks, collars, binds, fetters, handcuffs and whips of the land, washes until those wounds belong to the sea.

Water caresses the skin unloved on land for so long. Water applies its soft salted lips to every pore of that body in an attempt to enliven the very body it has wrestled to a stillness in the first place, as if the body's very surrender is a point of departure for water from conqueror to worshipper. Sea refuses to grant that body the quiet of a grave in the ground. Instead it rolls that body across its terrain, sends that body down into its depths, its stellar dark, swells the body to bursting point, tumbles it beyond the reach of horizons and gradually breaks fragments from that body with its nibbling, dissecting current.

Soon all those bodies melt down to bones, then the sea begins to treat the bones like rock, there to be shaped over time or ground to dust. Sea does not stop at death. Salt wants to consume every morsel of those bodies until the sea becomes them, becomes their memory. So it is from the sea that all 131 souls are to be plucked. From a sea oblivious to time. One hundred and thirty-one dissipated bodies find breath in the wind skimming the surface of the sea and howl. Those bodies have their lives written on salt water. The sea current turns pages of memory. One hundred and thirty-one souls roam the Atlantic with countless others. When the wind is heard it is their breath, their speech. The sea is therefore home.

The one-hundred-and-thirty-second lives far inland: can never set foot on water again, never look at an expanse of water wider than a river bridgeable with a pelted stone. Air is her conqueror, water theirs. Air is her preserver, water theirs. Air and water share the same earth, the same sea, the same sky. Both are consumed by fire. Sometimes a savannah will start to tumble bundles of bracken across its flat face and suddenly, through some

4

trick of the light and heat, it will tremble into a seascape and that bracken will become tossed into a sea current and this one-hundred-and-thirty-second body will have to be a witness again.

I

Chapter One

T HE *Zong* dug through the sea, steady and noisy as a
rocking chair over loose floorboards, and when the
sails thwacked from time to time to a sudden crosswind,
everyone on board heard – except those buried deep
below deck – an amplified sound like that of perfume
being slapped on to a just-shaved face.

Captain Cunningham emerged from his cabin and
peered at the dawn-lit sky and his assembled crew with
the squint he reserved for reading. Whatever he saw in the
bunched men and thick grey clouds speckled blue, drew
the frown he ordinarily deployed against untidy writing
or unrealistic instructions from an investor. He used his
right hand to stroke the left side of his face, partly to
clarify his thinking and partly to enjoy the smoothness
of a recent shave. His middle finger settled on the dimple
in his chin that was always so difficult to defoliate and
searched it. How to begin? he wondered. With a deep
breath mostly of salt spray air and a wisp of the perfume
on his face he answered himself, 'At the beginning, of
course.' He acknowledged the smiling face of his first
mate, Kelsal, with a sharp nod. Kelsal's smile switched
to a pursed-lipped stare, his more familiar demeanour.

All swayed in unison, like a church choir, in opposition to the steady locomotion of the ship. More than the wind in the sails and the sea against the sides or the strain in the ship's timbers plummeting through water were the just audible cries emanating from below decks. But neither the captain nor the assembled crew seemed to hear them, or perhaps, like the sea, the ship and the sails, these cries had grown so habitual to the sailors' ears, they were no longer heard as signals of distress, but as part of the whole, all-encompassing fabric of routine.

Captain Cunningham planted his knuckles in his hips. As if spurred by the action, he immediately raised his chest and shoulders, jutted his chin forward so that he was at his full height, sucked a generous portion of air akin to a shot of rum bolted down to give backbone to some otherwise tenuous resolve, and began.

'Gentlemen, we have a complication of such potentially disastrous consequences for our investments that the solution requires of us all a degree of brass courage.' Several nods and hear, hears, in agreement, pleased him. A few quizzical looks from the lesser hands, he could afford to ignore, so he resumed.

'We have surrendered seven good men to these waters and lost thirty-six of our holdings. I do not intend to bury another. One-twelfth of our holdings lost! With each loss our commission dwindles. These three months of hard work, sacrifice and suffering will come to nothing. We must act decisively or return to our families and friends and investors empty-handed. Which is it to be, gentlemen?'

Captain Cunningham paused. He expected to hear unanimous calls of 'Profit! Profit!' Instead, he faced confused expressions and indecipherable grumbles. The men seemed to think he had posed the question, not for an answer from them, but to himself as part of a larger elucidation that was bound to follow his long pause. The captain fought back an impulse to shout, 'Which is it to be, gentlemen?' at them again. They watched him with varying degrees of concentration etched on their faces. Some shrugged. He pressed his knuckles deeper into his hips to avoid punching the face of the nearest sailor and thereby knocking some common sense into the visage or at least dislodging the mask of attentiveness and revealing the stupidity that languished underneath. What he summoned was the patience he needed in massive reserves to deal with sailors and slaves.

'Are we to make a loss or a profit? Which is it to be, gentlemen?' This time the appropriate cries of 'Profit! Profit!' were elicited from them. He waited for the discussion that erupted to subside. First Mate Kelsal shushed at a few of the more talkative men nearby, which had the desired effect of returning the focus to the captain.

Kelsal's permanent pleat of skin between his eyebrows, coupled with his pursed lips, conferred on him the unusual aspect of someone who was always listening intently. Looking at him there would be no way of telling he was unsure where the captain's mind and obvious resolve would lead them next. Wherever it led he knew he would have to follow, as he had always followed, since every reasonable path was preferred to this stagnation of death and disease which had gripped the *Zong* and brought it to the brink of failure and anchored it there for weeks, in this, its last African mission. Ten weeks at sea and the prospect of the horizon yielding up the land that they believed was there, of land alongside instead of perennial sea, was still a dream. First the slaves became sick. This was expected. But with each death and no end in sight, fear spread among the twenty-four members of the crew that their turn would come. The ship's doctor had succumbed, panic spread. He died. One after another the crew fell in with the vomiting and diarrhoea of the slaves, robbing the ship of hands that were vitally needed and the remaining crew of its will, souring the mission's hitherto delicious promise of wealth for all involved.

The captain savoured the moment. Everyone was silent. All eyes were trained on him. He gulped air as if rinsing out his mouth with it and resumed.

'The insurers' interests are at odds with ours. That you know. What you don't know is that every time a piece of cargo is lost we, not the insurers, must bear that loss, *unless* the loss is a measure taken by us to ensure against further depletion of our stocks. What I am about to propose, gentlemen, is one such measure to preserve this ship and the remainder of its holdings so that we may recover our losses from the insurance.'

'What further losses, Captain?'

Kelsal's question sought some clarification from the captain, who, believing Kelsal to be needlessly obtuse and obstructive, rounded on him.

'My first mate appears to be having some problems of comprehension. It appears that his proximity to the stock of this business has corrupted his common sense.' There were deferential grunts from the men.

'Sorry, Captain.'

Usually, when Kelsal spoke to the captain, he represented the thoughts and feelings of the rest of the crew. They deferred to him, seeing him as the only man in a position to question the captain's motives, or at least to seek more information from a captain they saw as too sparse in his praise and too thrifty with the details of his thinking, treating both as if they were scarce resources or stock about to run out on board ship and therefore in need of dire rationing. Even in disaster the captain maintained this parsimonious decorum and left the men mostly uninformed and more inclined to doubt and dissent than if they had been furnished with the facts of the matter.

'Let me repeat myself for the sake of my first mate. I suggest we divest ourselves of all the sick and infirm among our holdings on board this ship as a necessary measure to preserve the remainder of the cargo. Am I clear, First Mate Kelsal?'

Kelsal's features trembled. If it was possible to gather more skin between his eyes and project his lips further, he managed it, changing his concentration to consternation.

'You mean to get rid of the sick and infirm cargo, Captain?'

'Hooray, Kelsal is with us, gentlemen!' More conciliatory titters.

'Sir, we are talking of upwards of a hundred slaves.'

'And numerically endowed!' Soundless grimaces now.

'But how, Captain?'

'How, First Mate Kelsal? How?'

'Yes, sir, how?'

This was better than the captain could have hoped for. A modicum of resistance made it easier for him to be explicit and make his argument with some force. But he had to suppress this emergent levity in his tone and get his reasoning to sound more like a serious command.

'You are correct to ask about the logistics of this plan of mine, perfectly correct. You cannot read my mind, can you, Kelsal? I apologise. Let me explain.'

He surveyed his depleted crew, now down to seventeen, wishing one or two of the stragglers were among the seven dead, instead of the random way death had claimed some

13

of his most conscientious sailors as if a more important ship had to be staffed with reliable souls at the expense of the *Zong*'s efficiency. Where had his first mate found them all anyway, other than in the alehouses of Liverpool and Manchester? Drinking from tankards refilled at no cost to themselves and entertaining the notion of the sea in the dregs at the bottom of their mugs that had to be refilled again, until the idea of a voyage swelled inside and swilled about in their distended bellies and they incorporated it into some lewd song – spurred on no doubt by Kelsal's propensity for lyrics that emulated the profane, and by yet another refill, fancied themselves at sea and so had to be carried out of the pub to sign with whatever mark they could make to represent their inebriated consent.

'First Mate Kelsal will supervise the identification of the sick and infirm among our holdings. They will be brought on deck in small numbers and then thrown over the side . . .'

Captain Cunningham was forced to stop here on account of the men's gasps at his revelation. He began again in a raised and breathless voice and hurried to the finish.

'To ensure, gentlemen, the health and survival of the remainder. Our health and survival too, I might add.'

The murmurings continued, and from Kelsal's grossly contorted features and parted lips they spelled disbelief. The captain interjected with 'Water supplies are low.' Intended, no doubt, to clinch his argument, it served merely to delay an overflow of dissent.

'Gentlemen, need I remind you of the ruin facing each of us unless we can turn a profit?' He looked at Kelsal for assistance.

'There must be another way, Captain.'

Kelsal's plea was welcomed as something specific to address. 'If there was some other solution, Kelsal, don't you think I would have thought of it?'

A sudden change in the direction of the wind leaned the ship to starboard forcing everyone to grasp the nearest thing that was fastened to the deck. The captain grabbed on to Kelsal in an instinctive gesture to prevent himself falling, and without any thought for his own safety Kelsal offered what support he could but was forced by the ship's sharp lean to fall to one knee. Then the boom of the mainmast swung and a few heads ducked. Along with creaking wood and some loose items crashing to the deck, shouts and screams climbed up the stairs leading from below and escaped through the barred hatches or else managed to squeeze through the grooves between the planks of the upper deck. A righted ship did nothing to quell them.

Captain Cunningham released his grip on Kelsal, jerked both arms forward to adjust his jacket and waited for his crew to settle. Kelsal stood up solemnly as if he'd just been knighted. His bevelled shoulders disguised his true height with a pronounced stoop. This, combined with his stern stare, added menace to his demeanour. The *Zong* straightened from the surprise blow to its port side. The sea towered above the side of the ship and leapt on to the deck and splashed everyone, and from being relatively dry a moment ago, each man now stood dripping and clearing strands of hair from his eyes. A few spat at their feet, obviously trying to rid their mouths of the salt spray, and as was the habit of barefoot men who didn't want to hinder the progress of their mates across an already treacherous deck, used their soles to clear the spit away by spreading it thinly over a wide area with sweeping motions of the feet.

'We will ensure only the sick and infirm are disposed of in this way. First Mate Kelsal will lead a delegation of you in the task of selecting and jettisoning. I will be on deck to oversee matters. This is a problem for the insurers to resolve, not for us to suffer. There are 408 slaves remaining. If we dispose of one third, at £39 a head from the insurance and from the sale of the remainder we stand to make a clear profit in this venture, as is our right after months of investment of our energies. Dismissed.'

The men broke away from the gathering into smaller groups of twos and threes. Earnest discussions in hushed tones ensued. A few felt that this was asking too much of them since they were sailors first and foremost, not soldiers of fortune.

'They are primitive people, but still people.'

'I've seen some in Liverpool who are baptised.'

'And in London.'

The majority did not mind carrying out the order – 'They are stock,' 'Cargo,' 'As delicate as horses and calves but chattel all the same!' – but felt that the premise itself was too far-fetched to convince the insurers of its necessity. What if the insurers refused to pay? Then there would be nothing to show for all their efforts, nothing for all their sacrifice, nothing to assuage their consciences.

They asked First Mate Kelsal for his opinion. He was tough but always seemed attentive and thoughtful to the world around him. What Kelsal recommended, they would accept, whatever the outcome. They waited. Kelsal looked at the captain for permission to address them. Consent was granted by the captain with an emphatic nod. Kelsal sighed. Another moment when he had to follow the captain's command presented itself. Like all orders, this one tasted like the sea: unpalatable and unavoidable under the circumstances. He avoided the men's searching looks by keeping his eyes fixed on the horizon. He cursed its unbroken line: there was no other course but to proceed. In the distance that it kept, the horizon appeared to challenge him to behave differently. But Kelsal's only recourse was obedience, however questioning. He directed his stare at whoever among the men was willing to lock eyes with him and, finding no one up to the task who lasted more than a second before looking away – not even his second mate – he realised he would have to speak his mind without any support.

'You heard the orders from our venerable captain, gents. Orders are orders, and when they come from a good captain such as Captain Cunningham they are considered and therefore likely to result in our good fortune. I say we rid this vessel of its sick and infirm to protect ourselves and guarantee our profit. What say you?'

There were traces of dismay on the faces of the men, one or two shook their heads negatively, but the verbal assent was unanimous, 'Aye, ayes' flying back and forth among the crew. Drifting blackened cloud overhead had stitched over the last patches of blue peeping between gaps in this heavy, dark drape spread in the heavens. A final rumble of satisfaction, from a machinist who had completed a thankless task, rolled across the black covers. Sailors reputed to smell fresh water before it fell had the more reliable evidence of their eyes and ears on this occasion. Those clouds and that thunder could only mean a downpour was imminent. They raced to furl the fore-, main- and mizzen-topsails, batten down the hatches, open water storage barrels, hide powder and shot under tarpaulin and protect matches and oiled torches from the open air. Two crewmen, instead of the usual one, had to steady the long whipstaff that controlled the rudder.

Others even grabbed soap in their eagerness to enjoy a shower in fresh water.

Captain Cunningham called them to attention.

'All hands attend me here now! First Mate Kelsal!'

Kelsal was first by the captain's side. 'Captain?'

Captain Cunningham waited for the stragglers, as he called them – the last to assemble, the first to break for food, the last to rise to their duties, the first to run from them – to come within earshot before he spoke.

'You misunderstand me, gentlemen. I mean for us to begin the execution of these orders now. This moment. Before we turn to any other task, however pressing. None can be as pressing as this.' The captain wondered what Kelsal and the rest of the crew could have been thinking. That with the decision would come some period of adjustment to the idea before the actual following through with it? Feeding the stock their final meal of the day was at 4 p.m., less than two hours away. Rations would be saved if the next two hours were passed disposing of as many mortally sick as the crew could lay hands on. He let them know his mind on the matter and called on Kelsal.

'First Mate Kelsal, select a party to accompany you below. Start with the severest cases. Pass me here so I can see and record each one. Dispose of the stock to starboard. Come on, men, move along, you're not salt, a few drops of rain won't hurt you.'

Captain Cunningham looked at Kelsal and jerked his head towards the hatch leading down to the lower deck where the slaves were chained. Kelsal paused, looked up at the blackened sky for some divine intervention that he seemed to believe ought to be forthcoming, looked in turn at the captain one last time with a slight expectation that this bluff would be called off and the more usual routines of running a ship would be restored to one and all, got no such reprieve so, pointing out three of the best crew, proceeded to unbar the hatch to below.

Kelsal turned his face away from the hot stench that greeted him as the hatch was lifted. The air had thickened with sweat from bodies that had not been allowed to wash for days but which had sweated in stale, airless confinement where the temperatures alone would cause a body to break into a dripping sweat without the slightest activity on its part. Add to this the accident of vomit from the sick, urine from those chained for such inordinately long spells that even the most accommodating bladders would rebel, add, too, the fact that if at one of the day's two meals adults and children had not used the buckets allocated to them for human waste, for whatever reason, constipation or a lack of inclination, or just sheer lack of opportunity (before the orders and rough treatment resumed as their jailers sought to fasten them to their chains and bolts in record time so that they themselves could escape an atmosphere too rank for the toughest constitution among them), then they were left to stew in their faeces.

Howls, moans, cries, calls and implorings in indecipherable tongues assailed Kelsal's ears. He held his lantern forward into the dreary space to pick out lame from able-bodied but could not distinguish between man and man. All seemed one miserable, tangled mass of humanity. A sea of eyes, flesh welded into one body of complaints, on occasion separating into distinct entities of mankind, but mostly indistinguishable one from another as anything but a sound, a movement, a plea inscribed on some face momentarily by a lamp, before melting back into the thick dark. Kelsal saw the Africans' continued survival under such adverse circumstances as evidence of their suitability for a life of unremitting toil.

But the fact of so many sick and dying had to be reckoned with too. And he was here to identify the severest cases when any picked at random would easily qualify as such.

'Take hold of him.'

Two of the crewmen moved to a man lying with his head in his arms and unshackled the anklet that linked him to another man, who cowered from the stick held at the ready. The man was dragged to his feet and pushed towards the steps leading to the main deck. He had difficulty walking, a combination of stiff limbs, cramps and plain weakness. Two sailors got hold of each of his arms and, because of the lack of room to manoeuvre, propelled him towards the exit in a sideways motion. The third sailor unshackled another man, who lay quite still as if asleep and who hardly stirred when prodded in the ribcage with a club. His companion in chains helped him to rise to one knee then uttered words of encouragement to him in a tongue that sounded to Kelsal's ears like a nonsensical tune mouthed to soothe a teething infant. Others around him were alert by now and they too spoke words of consolation or else castigated him for his slowness. Whichever, he made a mighty effort to get to one knee and the crewman with the club cursed him for his slowness and used a free hand to drag him to his feet. Many slaves barely lifted their heads to look.

Kelsal could see there would be numerous sick to choose from. He could hear children crying in their compartment a little way off. And farther away the distress calls of women. He spun around to catch up with the crewmen escorting the lame slaves. He was more than relieved to be getting back to the fresh air. Only what he heard next could have kept him below decks a moment longer. He froze.

'Kelsal!'

He listened and turned his head slowly in the direction he believed the call came from even though it seemed incredible to him that its origin was even deeper in this miserable cavern. No, he thought, I am hearing things. He moved towards the exit again but had taken less than two steps when the call came again, this time clearer and a little more impatient.

'Kelsal!'

Now he was certain that it came not from the hatch, where only one man used his name in such a commanding tone, but from deep inside this dungeon. He stopped and turned, raised his lantern to shoulder height to increase its circumference of illumination but was forced to lower it once more when the flame began to dim and flicker from lack of oxygen. Kelsal looked back in the direction of the hatch where the crewman waited impatiently for his prevaricating first mate to join him and decided against investigating the source of the call for the moment.

'I'll be back,' he shouted into the darkness to his right where he thought the culprit lay shackled. From his uncertain steps and the way he glanced back periodically it was clear he wanted to investigate the matter right away, rather than supervise the proper disposal of the sick slaves.

Kelsal was glad to be back in the open. He found his nostrils and mind were as attentive to the salt spray air as though to some expensive perfume. He drank it in with deep breaths. Two of the crew, their faces contorted from their exposure to the atmosphere below, closed and barred the hatch.

Both slaves were presented to the captain, who opened a ledger which he shielded against the light rain that had just begun and made two strokes in it. He turned to

Kelsal and spoke in a loud voice clearly intended for all to hear.

'If you were a gambling man, First Mate Kelsal, how long would you give these two pieces of cargo?'

Kelsal was surprised by the question. He looked at the captain then turned to estimate for himself just how sick these two holdings appeared in the dull afternoon light that actually seemed very strong after a spell below deck. Both squinted and stood with a pronounced stoop clasping their arms around their midriffs. One was unsteady on his feet on account of the ship's sway and his weakness. He seemed about to tumble over in any direction. The second man shifted his weight from one leg to another as if the deck beneath him were hot, then he fell to his knees. The sailors nearest to him tried to drag him back up, but Kelsal motioned to them to leave him. The first man swayed so far to the left that he tumbled on to his rump. Kelsal noticed that no attempt was made by him to break his fall. Both arms remained wrapped around his stomach. How much life is in them? he wondered. A day? Two? He wanted to look closer at their faces. A face doesn't lie about things like death.

He dropped to one knee beside the man who had collapsed on all fours. By placing the back of his hand under the chin and applying a gentle upward pressure Kelsal lifted the bowed head. He could tell by the relaxed neck muscles that there was no resistance, yet the man's head felt incredibly heavy. Now for the eyes. Kelsal searched them. They were half-closed or half-open. And dark. The whites were rust-brown and the irises black, and even lifted skywards they appeared drained of light, empty somehow and dry. Not like eyes at all. Barely a day, he thought. He shifted to the other man, who was seated, and was about to lift the chin as he'd done before when the man looked up at him. These eyes were black, too, and the whites were brown, no, muddy. They were half-closed but not through lack of will. These eyes were contracted against something. They were lubricated eyes, like two marbles dipped in oil. Eyes in pain.

'A day or two, Captain Cunningham.'

The captain nodded with satisfaction. 'Knowing this, First Mate Kelsal, that in a day or two our holdings will be depleted by two at our expense, and two days of food and water squandered, do you not see my solution as manifest economic sense?'

'Yes, Captain.'

'Then over the side with them, man. To starboard.'

Kelsal looked at his crew and waved them towards the two men seated and kneeling on the deck.

'You heard the captain. One of you on each arm and leg and swing them over starboard.'

The closed fists of clouds opened and the rain intensified. Large drops were sown on the deck with the sound of little kisses. Both slaves raised their heads and opened their mouths. The slave on his knees unwrapped one arm from his stomach and held it palm upwards to collect drops. His eyes were closed. The slave who was seated opened his eyes wide so that the rain fell directly on them, then he fell on his back and his arms slackened around his belly.

The crewmen waited, unsure what to do next. The collapsed slave was breathing with difficulty, pulling in air that his nostrils had to hunt to locate. His companion looked at him and then at Kelsal.

'Damn it! What are these men waiting for, Kelsal, Christmas?'

'Sorry, Captain. Right, men, you have your orders. Over the side with them.'

23

There were only a few feet between the sailors and the two slaves, but they seemed unable to close the gap and pick up the slaves as ordered. They were looking at Kelsal, perhaps only believing an order of this nature if it was demonstrated by him or at least if he participated in carrying it out. The captain shook his head in dismay.

Kelsal grabbed the slave who had fallen over by peeling one arm from his stomach. 'Well, come on, you stragglers, I'm not doing it by myself.'

Three of the crew ran forward. Each took a limb. They looked at each other and at Kelsal and marched to starboard, and as they neared the side picked up speed to a trot, and at the side lifted the African up in the air and flung him at the rain and the sea. They looked over the side but Kelsal turned away. The slave on his knees tried to get to his feet. Four more crewmen grabbed him. They had difficulty moving together since he appeared to struggle even in his weak condition. But their tightened grips and swiftness in completing the task made the slave's struggle look perfunctory. They ran with him to the side and, as he shouted, hoisted him into the air and flung him over. For a moment he looked to be stuck against the canvas of air and rain and sea, his arms clawing and his legs kicking for familiar ground. A soundless splash and he was gone as if he had never knelt before them.

'Get some more. Hurry it up, gentlemen.'

The captain had his ledger shielded under his cloak. He looked up and mouthed a curse at the unburdening heavens and huddled in a cove between the main deck and quarterdeck just out of reach of the rain dropping in ribbons from above.

Kelsal thought he heard his name shouted. Not as a command but in anger.

'Kelsal!'

He glanced at the captain, who stood in the opposite direction from where he knew the sound originated. The captain was still absorbed in protecting his precious ledger from the rain that not only fell vertically but slanted too, even horizontally and, furthermore, seemed able to turn corners. Kelsal looked at the hatch where his name had seeped out and then at one or two of the crew nearby who appeared to be waiting on him but who had not heard his name shouted. The smattering of water on the deck, the susurrations of rain on the sea, the smacks of the sea itself against the hull as the ship dipped and rose and rocked to and fro, and the wood of the ship complaining about being pulled this way and that, seemed more than sufficient to drown any other sound. But not to Kelsal's ears tuned to his name.

The wind was blowing harder now, picking up apace. It filled the mainsail and the seven lesser sails. The rain pelted them, so much rain that they appeared sodden. Kelsal could see that a couple of the smaller sails, if not the mainsail itself, needed to be reefed in.

'Captain.'

'Yes, Kelsal, I know your mind. Attend to the sails.'

Kelsal fired commands and four men clambered up the main rigging. Climbing together they could be mistaken for a spider ascending the ship or leaving its central position on its web for the uppermost point in order to retrieve a trapped prey. The smaller sails were managed from the deck by pairs of sailors who manipulated long ropes, reefing them, to reduce the surface area of each sail to safer proportions.

The heavy rain had woven its web over everything, dividing the world into segments and obscuring a good deal of it too. Now the wind intensified. Before, it was merely playing in the sails and rigging, in the sleeves, trouser-legs and shirts of the men. Now it had found a voice that was a hum around the mainmast and whistled through the ship's rigging and rose to a howl, drowning out rain, sea and the distress that rose from below, putting in its place those very voices locked deep in the hull, up on to the deck, up into the rigging, up among the sails and all around the ship, in a chorus of lamentation from which there was no hiding place, no door to be slammed, no hatch barred and no stopper coarse enough to protect the ears.

The quietest place was now the kennels down below. When the slaves heard a complaint louder than their own they listened. Their voices had become detached from them, no longer reliant on the capacity of their lungs, adding to this big engine that powered itself and understood their countless reasons for giving it expression, and grew on this understanding into an independent force so powerful now it was capable of wrecking the vessel where it was born.

The sea was nowhere and everywhere. Africa was grief to them. Numberless villages flung inland from its coast. Village squares were empty, huts vacant. Acres of land had gone neglected, accountable to the hands and feet chained below. Livestock wandered without being herded by their calls and whistles. Loyed ones had been lost to those hearts. Those chests hurt so much, each was fit to burst under the weight and pressure. Bodies had gone from strokes of love only and the labour of love, to lashes and cuts and bruises, chains and collars. And from dances in the arms of lovers, from dances at harvest, at births, at deaths, from drums, strings, flutes and horns, they had come to this: a confined hole where to twist a little encumbered another, where elbows on each side speared into ribs and sleep was light, patchy, eyes wide, fitful, snatched, troubled, whimpering.

The voice above deck knew Africa and how this sea was nowhere and how their destination was not a beginning but an end without ending. That if the sea came to an end and another land suggested itself to them they would be lost forever but not dead, lost but never to be found. And love would be nowhere: behind them and impossible to recover; a flat line in the wake of the ship where the sky bowed down to the sea or the sea ascended to the sky. Love was lost somewhere in the very sea with its limitless capacity to swallow love, slaves, ships, memories. And so they had to send their voices into the air. Not the sea. Every stale breath was drawn to this end. Their voices dislodged the dirt packed between the planks of the deck and found the open and gathered in the heavens.

They were quiet now. They listened. Two among them had been taken and not returned. Not removed like the dead over these weeks had to be removed but taken alive and treated like dead. What else could come down on their heads? Hadn't every bad thing happened that could possibly happen? This new thing with the two who had not returned would outstrip everything they had encountered so far. They could tell from the voice above deck that was louder and more troubled than anything they had dreamed.

'Kelsal!'

Kelsal heard his name again. The moment the sails were furled he formed two delegations to descend into the slave quarters. He grabbed a club and stowed it in his waistband. The crewmen opened the hatch with their necks extended to one side and their faces averted to avoid the blast of foul air from the hold. The half-doors were secured to the deck and the men queued to descend the stairs, bending with each step to match the lowered roof. Once below they headed for the nearest sick quarry. But Kelsal ordered them to move deeper down the aisles and to be silent and listen for English.

'English, Mr Kelsal?'

'You heard. English.'

Three men accompanied Kelsal down one aisle and four others kept abreast of them down a parallel aisle a few feet away. They were near the end of the space allotted to males when the voice sounded again.

'Kelsal!'

This time everyone down below with Kelsal heard it. Kelsal looked around at them and saw the astonishment on their faces. He felt the blood rush up his neck and fill his head. He drew his club from his belt and gripped it tight. Then he stopped and gestured for everyone to be especially attentive now. They were near but the darkness made it hard to see more than a few feet ahead. Nothing. Kelsal bashed the roof with his club and cursed under his breath.

'Kelsal!'

The voice did not belong to any of the men chained to each other and fastened to the deck all around. It came from the female section. Kelsal rushed at the partition between the male and female quarters and squeezed through the small gap in it. He passed his club behind him and thrust his lantern into the face of a woman to his left. She stared up at him and said accusingly, 'Kelsal!' Her eyes were wet. She bared her teeth at him. Kelsal's lantern dimmed and went out due to lack of air. He couldn't tell if she was smiling or angry. He grabbed a handful of her coarse, unkempt hair.

'So you know my name. Unshackle her and take her up.'

'Kelsal, where are those two men?'

Her English was heavily accented but clear. She stood about five inches shorter than Kelsal and seemed to him to be about eighteen or twenty years of age. Her large eyes glistened as if they retained the flame of his failed lamp. The crewmen felt around her feet, found her ankles and unlocked her from the woman beside her. She was slow getting to her feet. Kelsal pushed her ahead of him and spoke to her back as they progressed to the hatch in that stooped walk that was required to save the head from knocking against the deck above them.

'Where did you learn English?'

'At a Christian mission.'

He wondered about the location of the mission but, without quite knowing why, he was reluctant to display an inordinate interest in her in the presence of so many of the crew.

'Why did you not impart this to us weeks ago?'

'What would you have done with me? Set me free?'

Kelsal again felt his temper rising. He was inclined to hit her on the head with his club in that instant but thought it best to show her to the captain.

The moment she stepped out of the hold she felt the wind and the rain. Both lifted her spirits. She threw her head back as far as it would go and opened her mouth wide. Water and air were one delicious condiment to her palate. Her eyelids fluttered to stay apart and allow her to look, despite being pummelled by the rain, as though the air might reveal itself to her at any moment as the rain had done, rain she knew but hadn't seen or felt for a long time and so had come to doubt, air that had now taken shape as an invisible body pressing on her upturned face.

Kelsal explained to the captain that the woman knew English and had been shouting his name in a manner to provoke him but, more importantly, one that was likely to incite rebellion in the other slaves.

'You like my first mate's name?'

The captain, still clutching his ledger under his cloak, joined the small party of men surrounding the woman.

'What are you called?'

He spoke with a deliberate loudness, believing perhaps that she was hard of hearing.

'What is your tribe? Your name? Your tribe?'

She looked at them through the wet ribbons that clothed her naked body. Kelsal stood next to the captain, brandishing his club at chest level, almost as a shield against the rain.

'I am Fetu. I am called Mintah. I was captured by slavers after the Dutch destroyed the Danish mission.'

Kelsal's jaw dropped in disbelief. Her words reverberated in his head.

'Good for you, Mintah. You need some exercise, some discipline. Don't you think she needs some exercise, gentlemen?'

The majority of the crew cheered in the affirmative. Captain Cunningham continued, 'Dance for us, Mintah. Dance.'

Kelsal hardly heard any of this. He simply mimicked the antics and sounds of everyone around him as they responded to the captain while he stared at Mintah, putting all of his energy into ransacking his past to see if he could produce an image from it that approximated to the young woman facing him.

The captain produced a whip and lashed at Mintah's feet. She skipped to avoid the blow but it stung her calves. Kelsal and the bow-legged second mate began to clap their encouragement, Kelsal bringing one end of his club crashing into his open palm, and the captain took this as his cue to crack his whip again at Mintah's feet. She screamed and jumped and kept moving to avoid drawing another whiplash. More of the crew joined in the clapping, which synchronised into a rough beat for Mintah to dance to. They were watching her, but their thoughts were preoccupied with what she had said. Most of them knew that time spent at a mission meant she was not like the other slaves. Her prolonged contact with missionaries amounted to a familiarity with whites. The missionaries' civilising zeal did not stop at saving the heathen soul. She would have gained an education, would be able to read and write, when most of them could barely sign their names. She would have learned about the kind of world they came from. All of which took the place of the usual fear of whites and resulted in a slave who was difficult to subjugate.

Mintah decided to dance the death of fertility dance. Fertility's temporary death and eventual rebirth. No doubt they would see it as her willingness to obey their every whim, but she *needed* to dance this particular dance. Had gone through its details in her head over the last thirty-six hours, most of which she'd spent chained below decks lying on her right side without enough room to sit up, barely able to turn over without lying on someone else, and seeing in her mind's eye her body dancing this very dance in a village square with dust raised by her feet and the dust-stockinged feet of other young women, and sand grains clinging to the sweat on their bodies and their long, flickering shadows cast by the fires stretching into the dark and the drums resounding on the thick walls of the night. Now here was her chance. To transfer the pain of the whip around her legs to that of her womb. To placate the fertility god. To touch imaginary soil with the balls of her foot, bow her head, contract her shoulders and throw her open palms to the heavens in half-steps that would complete a circle of her own following the direction of the moon, a circle within the circle made by these alien men. And be cleansed by the rain, by water in its purest form, direct from the well of the gods, not flowing in a river, nor stored in the ground, nor made manifest at dawn as droplets on grass or pooled in the cups of leaves, but pelting, lashing, licking tongues of rain. Mintah replaced the crew's clapping with drums. She looked up at the sky or at her feet, no longer seeing these men. Her ears filled with the wind, rain, her heart and the balls of her feet on the deck.

Captain Cunningham shouted above the clapping, stamping and the storm, 'Our dear surgeon, God rest his soul, did say exercise was good for the stock. Right, Kelsal?'

Kelsal, stooping towards the captain, had inclined his ear towards him and was nodding with a blank mind and a broad smile. He answered, 'Yes, Captain,' mechanically.

Mintah stopped and looked at the captain and Kelsal. Her eyes were narrowed.

'I am baptised like you.'

The clapping stopped. Captain Cunningham stamped his right heel on the deck.

'Watch your tongue, woman!' He thrust his whip at Kelsal. 'Remind this female of her station, then return her to the hold.'

He glared at Mintah and left the deck for his quarters, clutching his ledger tightly under his right arm.

Kelsal waited for the door to close behind the captain. He pushed Mintah to the ground and asked the crew to restrain her. The boatswain knelt before her and began to unbuckle his trousers. Kelsal pushed him away from her so hard that the man fell on his side and looked up at Kelsal astonished. Rain on the deck pooled red between Mintah's thighs. Kelsal saw her menstrual blood. The boatswain cursed and stood up. Disappointment marked his face. There would be another time, he consoled himself.

'Turn her over,' Kelsal ordered.

The men pulled Mintah on to her stomach and kneeled on her arms and held her splayed ankles. Kelsal kicked the whip that he had dropped at his feet further away and grabbed his club. He began to beat Mintah on her shoulders. She screamed. He shifted his attention to her back then down to her bottom, then her legs, working his way up one side of her body and down the other. She screamed, and shouted his name, begging him to spare her. And when Kelsal hit her left kidney for the second time as he methodically beat his way up her body, she saw water spinning on the deck, with the grain in the wood rearranged from straight lines into a vortex with a dark point at its centre that expanded into concentric circles until it grew into the entire deck, filling her head with soundlessness and blackness.

'She's out, Mr Kelsal.'

There was an urgency in the second mate's tone. A certain dissatisfaction with having to hold the female down for this conclusion: her limp body, her quiet. Kelsal saw no purpose in beating her further if she did not know about it. He was inclined to have her revived and then resume the punishment. But the faces of the men around him, including his trustworthy second mate's, appeared to take little or no pleasure in the exercise. The men on either side of her restrained her effectively, but looked elsewhere and flinched with each blow as if a relative of theirs were the object of his attentions. If she had called their name

33

like she had called his, they would feel differently. They would probably have wanted to bludgeon her and throw her over the side. Of this he was certain. Nevertheless, he decided to rest.

Two crewmen dragged her back below, disgruntled that the show they had hoped to participate in had been curtailed; not Kelsal's pointless beating, but what the boatswain had been about to do and would have done had Kelsal not interfered. Breathing heavily and gripping his club with both hands, Kelsal pounded louder than he intended on the door of the captain's cabin and announced that they were ready to resume jettisoning the sick with his permission. The captain said he would join them presently and to proceed with bringing sick stock above deck; each deleted infirm piece restoring in his head, bit by bit, the original cornucopia promised by the ship's crowded hold.

Chapter Two

THE SEA TROUGHED and peaked, sending the *Zong* into steep ascents of shifting, sheer cliffs and then dropping the hull from those heights, not in progressively faster slides downhill, but by removing from under the *Zong* all support so that the ship crashed down precipice after precipice and slammed to a standstill, then climbed another incline, or was elevated up, only to be dumped over another peak as before. Water drummed against the hull, skittered over the sides, swilled into alcoves on decks, assembled in the neat coiled snakes of ropes and grew off awnings like bearded vines. Wind performed a maypole dance around the masts and bloated the bodies of the sails. How could land sit in this? Here the concept of land was as remote as the sun and the moon and the stars. Fixed points in the mind.

Clouds thickened and moved close to the bow and stern, billowed and dipped just beyond the reach of a rod, if that rod were extended by a curious hand over port or starboard. Mintah stirred. Her head hit the deck it lolled against a few times. She found herself on her right side as the surgeon had taught the crew to arrange slaves, 'to aid the unrestricted beating of

35

the heart'. She could hear his curmudgeonly barking of instructions as he shrugged his shoulders and shook his head as though he had already been disobeyed. He came to mind because she knew what he would have said if she had been brought before him. 'The best cure, young woman, is prevention. Not to bring calamity on your head by sending out invitations of insolence.' And he would have done nothing but have her returned to her slice of space below decks as if his reprimand were, in its own right, a prescription and remedy for her ailment. He was old and had grown sick like the others and died shrugging his shoulders and shaking his head to the end but without breath to power the vocal complaints that, doubtless, had been running through his head but had failed to connect with his disobedient tongue.

'This disease will run a short course. No need to panic.'

None of the crew had believed a word he'd said. And when he succumbed to the infection they despaired that any of them would live to see land again. But even in death he was right. It had indeed abated and the many sick were slowly gaining strength. There would be more deaths but no new cases. Why then had those two sick men been removed? She could not conceal her ability to speak English under these circumstances. Keeping it a secret had exposed her to little of value.

From what she had overheard in the eight weeks they had been at sea, Kelsal seemed the most reasonable among the ship's crew. He deliberated when the others simply reacted. There was the incident when an old man looked at the second mate's shoe and asked if it was made from the skin of African people and the second mate replied, 'Yes,' and laughed along with the captain and everyone else, while Kelsal waited for the laughter to die down, then quietly explained, to nods of approval from the surgeon and impatient shrugs at the continuing ribaldry, that this material was animal skin, cattle in fact, and that the old man, and the women, even the children, would be used to work the land. This seemed to satisfy the old man who told the others, though some of the more inquisitive and disbelieving among them wanted to know what manner of land was this that so many Africans were needed to work it.

Rumours persisted among a large number of slaves that these people would trade all of them in their markets as meat, a much sought after delicacy, with African bones ground to powder and used, like elephant tusks, for its sexual potency or ability to purge the blood, and black, soft, durable skin for clothes and shoes, belts and gloves. Mintah was adamant when faced with these stories. They would not be eaten, they would be sold as slaves to work the land. Their skin would not be used to make apparel for the whites but it had marked them out for this manner of forced labour. If not ground to dust, what would become of their bones? They would lie in unsanctified ground, ground untrodden by any ancestor, not laid to rest but left in limbo. Each spirit would have to find its way home over this sea, over a scattered road of bones.

Pain radiated from her back up her spine to her head. Was she thinking too hard on these matters? How could her assessment of Kelsal have been so wrong? He was cruel like the others and harboured the worst thoughts about her and her people just like his peers. Whatever reason he put to work was to bring about the smooth workings of the ship and nothing more. Reason was suspended by him when a black body said his name, and he saw it as impudence and sought not a fair punishment to bring redress, but revenge.

She heard the crew unshackle two sick women nearby. The women shouted her name as if she could reverse their fate. They were cuffed and kicked and dragged out of the hold provoking loud wails from the other women. Men called out the names of women. Children cried in their compartments for mothers who tried to reassure them. Among those children and men were two names that had been called which had remained unanswered, leaving a man in despair and an inconsolable child.

'Kelsal!'

His name burst out of her eyes and ears and nose and mouth. Her pores sweated his name. He seeped out from under her fingernails, from the ends of her hair. She saw herself taking hold of his hands, and she shouted his name at those hands for the offence of beating, for the offence of holding a living body and slinging it over the side into the uncaring sea, and the flesh peeled from those offending hands and the little, offending bones of the fingers and wrists splintered, shattered, crumbled and blew away. She shouted his name again, this time to his face, until his skin peeled off and his flesh and the bones in his face disintegrated followed by the rest of him.

Other crewmen returned and unshackled two more women, using their clubs to quell the cries around them by swinging randomly at the dark. The men cursed at their work. Their two new victims struggled and were hit and cried not from the blows but for the last look around them and for someone sequestered in that floating dungeon who depended on their love and presence. Their wails permeated the decks, competed with the wind and returned over the waves as swift as a migrant bird back to a village, town, hut, or embrace.

'Kelsal!'

Captain Cunningham marked the strokes in his ledger

and nodded with satisfaction. The crew worked with a minimum of words. Most of the sounds they made were from their exertions as they restrained the slaves. When they spoke it was to issue correctives to one another: 'Lift higher,' 'Don't let go now,' 'Help me with this leg,' 'Watch this one, she bites.' They coordinated their actions by counting three swings back and forth and flung the women away. What screams there were were muffled in thick spray and encroaching grey. They stared at each other to measure one another's stamina so far for the job, searching for the slightest trace of distaste that might appear in an expression.

'Get some children.'

The crew nodded and descended the hatchway to the children's quarters. One crewman whispered to his friend that it was not enough to kill the sick, then women – now they were to murder children. His friend agreed but urged him to keep his opinions to himself unless he wanted to invite the cat-o'-nine-tails on both their backs.

They searched for the quiet children, the least active ones. When they grabbed a child who was pretending to be asleep and he struggled against their hold they let him go and checked another in a similar state of apparent weakness. When he did not struggle much in their grown hands, although he had dedicated every fibre in his sick body to the enterprise, they took him above. Four of them were removed amid deafening shrieks from other children alert to their impending end and aware that there was no adult to intercede on their behalf.

Mothers shouted to children to show the evil men that they were not sick but healthy; to struggle and scream. Men banged their chains on the decks and shouted in Yoruba, Ewe, Ibo, Fanti, Ashanti, Mandingo, Fetu, Foulah, at the crew to leave the children and take them instead. Mothers pulled out their hair, fell into dead faints, wished for death to take them now, now, now, since life could never mean a thing after this. And cried with dry eyes and hardly a breath left in them.

Mintah thought about her performance above deck not so long ago. She felt ashamed. What fertility gods? Fructification for whose benefit? Her womb ached and her blood flowed for nothing. Her benediction to the gods was for what? None of it could save a single hair on the head of a child. She wanted her blood to run dry and for the intricate apparatus that she harboured inside to dislodge from its moorings and drift out of her; to expel it and never feel that particular pain again and never bleed for any god, for any dance.

Kelsal now appeared before Mintah with two crew members and chains. Mintah spat in his face. He lashed her twice about the head with his club. The two crewmen handcuffed her hands behind her back and chained both of her feet tightly. Kelsal took a kerchief from around his neck and gagged Mintah.

'Next time I will cut out your tongue!'

Then they left with two more women. One had fainted and came round as they dragged her out, and her struggle called forth blows from Kelsal's club and the men's fists and feet until she fell silent and compliant.

As soon as Kelsal was out of the hatch three more crewmen descended and selected another woman. She begged them to spare her and pointed to the children's quarters, indicating that she had a child to care for, but in their eyes she was sick. They dragged her away and her begging became screams. In an instant her weak body transformed into that of a mother separated from her child and she fought them. She screamed the child's name and the girl began to cry and call for her mother.

Distress spread to every corner of the compartment and enveloped it. Mintah could hear a commotion coming from the men's section too, mainly shouts and the sound of wood hitting flesh. The chains and the shouting became louder than the wind and the rain and the sea and the wood of the ship under the pressure of all three. She tried to see Kelsal's face in her mind. But his image refused to cohere and more dark than light moved about inside her head; circled, expanded and replaced all the light with unadulterated darkness.

'Why are they throwing us away?' Mintah was being shaken. The imploring voice echoed in her with the same question but a little louder with each repetition and echo. A hand was attempting to untie her gag. Mintah moved her head away and shook off the hand and pressed her forehead to the deck. The wood was hard, wet and warm. She had warmed it. Wet it also. Her skin had been shed here for ten weeks now: two waiting at the coast near the fort for the ship to reach its full complement; and eight at sea. The wood felt a part of her. To be truly like wood, indifferent to everything, grain fixed for all time, unchanging, she would have to be still, reduce her heavings in this stale, airless grave to nothing, be as still as wood, collect warmth, wet and shed skin, grow indifferent. She felt a knot in the wood right where her forehead lay. An impulse to look at it even in the dark was squashed by her. A knot in the wood meant grain had to swirl around it just as a boulder in a stream divided a current. Grain flowed around that knot. Was divided by it, but flowed around it nonetheless.

Even wood with all its indifference had its complaints. Didn't it moan and groan just like flesh and blood? Whipped, kicked and cursed by the sea? Not wood. She corrected herself. Grain. Her father loomed up from the grain, melted into her forehead and stood regarding her with his arms folded. She saw herself seated on the ground on a mud floor with a block of soft birch gripped between her feet. How small she seemed to herself. She was gouging chips from the birch in directions obedient to the flow of the grain. With each stroke she would look up at his face and he would nod and smile his encouragement. She would strike at the block a few more times. Then he would stoop down beside her and run his index finger along the grooves made by her chisel and nod more rapidly and happily. When he straightened again she'd resume. He was up there, way up there, how could he see what she saw up close? From all the way up there? Yet see he did, with those smiling eyes of his. Next time she looked up he'd be back at his own work, a few feet from her, a bigger block of wood, a hefty chisel she wasn't allowed to touch, seeking out the same runnellings of grain with little bursts of activity that curled shavings off and sweetened the air.

I will be grain, she thought. Grain around this knot of a voyage. Her father would look down at her, no, stoop down, run his finger over the smoothness of her and then straighten up pleased with the touch of her, approving of how she ran on the wood, around the knots, onward. Behind her father would be her mother. Her mother's round, smiling face and bosom that she loved to run up to and bury her face in, for its softness and sun-burnt smell. And behind her mother, their relations, and farther back friends and acquaintances, then the entire village and its animals, fields, trees and two rivers. And beyond the rivers the hills of Africa.

'Feeding time!' Cook bellowed. Crew members distributed themselves at equal intervals from below deck, and around the sides of the ship. Nets were draped down the sides at the main deck making it impossible for anyone to leap overboard. A man stood at a cannon on the quarterdeck while another shielded him with a piece of tarpaulin which was held up over a flame kept beside the cannon. Another was placed in a lookout station above the quarterdeck. He had a clear view of everyone and he shouted at a crew member closest to any of the slaves who seemed to behave out of the ordinary. First Mate Kelsal planted himself beside the captain next to a chest of loaded pistols, again shielded from the rain, and the rest of the crew held machetes and cutlasses in full view as additional deterrents to the slaves.

A crewman gave wooden bowls to each person as they emerged tentatively from the hatch into rain and wind. They squinted in the dull light. A meandering line formed towards a large vat that steamed with porridge. The cook cursed everyone and ladled a little less than one serving into the children's bowls, a full ladle into the women's and a full ladle plus a little extra into the men's. From his temper it was possible to believe he was giving away a personal fortune saved over a lifetime and not the odourless gruel passed off by him as food. He faced eternal abuse from the crew for his concoctions. Many of the ship's ailments were blamed on the often unidentifiable contents of his pot. When the surgeon was alive he took some of the abuse, but with his death the cook faced twice the invectives overnight. His intolerance had grown proportionately, even when he served the most ravenous slaves. The two exceptions were the captain and the first mate. Both were waited on by him with a sneer tucked away in the corner of his mouth and barely audible, respectful abbreviations of their names, 'Cap' and 'Kel'.

'Feeding time!' Cook frowned at the sick. His food was

wasted on them. They needed medicine or a miracle. He didn't want to have to look at them twice daily since they infected his eyes with a depression he found impossible to shake off. Why wait for them to die? He approved of the captain's decision to throw them overboard. What were all the arguments about among the crew? It was plain to see that these poor creatures were not yet fully formed humans. Their skin would have to become less dark, then white, their hair grow further from their skulls, and their lips and noses reduce to less prominent dimensions. They would wear more clothes. This much he knew.

Some of the men, women and children who were unable to walk unaided were herded by two crewmen to one side using the ends of their clubs to steer them. These sick were not given bowls. They sat on the deck and seemed oblivious to the drenching and the breeze. A couple revived and stood up, cured it seemed by their exposure to the elements. An older slave pointed them out to the crew distributing bowls and they were given wooden bowls and allowed to join the queue for food.

The captain spoke to Kelsal.

'Look at that bunch. Too sick even to eat. We should do something about them, First Mate.'

'After the cook has done serving the others, Captain?'

'No, Kelsal, now.'

Kelsal walked over to his second mate and the boat-swain.

'The captain said we should do something about those slaves who are too sick to eat.'

Both the second mate and the boatswain, from their expressions, seemed unsure what they were required to do, but only the second mate spoke up.

'We could get some of the healthy slaves to attend to them.'

'No. The captain means for us to dispose of them.'

The boatswain raised his eyebrows. A less restrained second mate spat on the deck in the vague direction of the captain.

'What? Now, Mr Kelsal?'

'Yes, Second Mate. Now.'

The second mate addressed the crew within earshot. After some argument about the appropriateness of the time, they stepped forward from their station along the sides and joined those crewmen responsible for separating the sick from the healthy. They lunged towards the nearest woman. She had reclined and rested her head on the leg of a man. They had not taken the time to agree about who would grab which part of her. This caused them to collide then battle over the same limb, releasing it at the same time then grabbing, simultaneously, at it again. And before a word could be said by the slaves who noticed, or any protest was registered by the woman, the crew had bundled her, in their uncertainty, to the side, grabbing and releasing her, so that she was dropped, dragged and carried in equal measure. Too many hands tried to lift her over the side: she was lifted higher than necessary and hurled hard through a hole in the net into the sea. More crew stepped forward with their guns and cutlasses and machetes and commanded the slaves to eat. Those who had turned from the vat with their bowls were lashed by the captain, who gesticulated to the cook to resume serving. The cook cursed loudly. First Mate Kelsal joined in the collecting up of the sick.

Four men scrambled to their feet and backed away from the rest of the sick who could barely lift their arms or kick at their assailants. Bowls were handed to the four while the pool of sick slaves that numbered about twenty dwindled as they were grabbed and hurled overboard, each one struggling and shouting to no avail.

Finally two children remained, a boy and girl about eight or nine years of age. They clung to each other and bawled, turning to the adults nearby for consolation.

What does death mean to a child of eight or nine? Adults who leave and never return. A friend who drowns in a river and is laid out all waxen and inert then placed underground, never to be seen again. A relative who hugged them one day and scolded them the next, around whom certain events took place, certain aromas abounded, a way of holding the arms, a particular stance, a recurring phrase, who suddenly stops and lies down, eyes closed impassively in a cold sleep, not the fitful sleep of the living, a death sleep. Death took something from the body of the living, stole from the living some vital thing. An eight- or nine-year-old body had this thing too. Besides a name, details of a face, besides a voice or breath. Death took this other thing that amounted to all of them put together and more. The boy and girl saw death all around them.

Now it appeared death had fixed its sights on their bodies, to deprive them of the thing that kept them in this world and transport them to its world of coldness, stillness, darkness. And going by the screams of adults, it appeared that death would hurt them as it snatched the life from them. So they cried and held each other.

Kelsal swivelled round from the net where he and another crew member had just discharged an older man, and watched as his second mate and the boatswain grabbed one child each. The two men moved towards the gap in the net at the same time, bumped into each other, stopped, and the boatswain bowed for the second mate to proceed with the boy, who was kicking and swinging his arms. He lifted the boy and swung him back as if about to hurl him into the onlooking slaves, but he kept his grip on the child and had just started to swing him forward and through the gap in the net when Mintah emerged from the hatch and screamed 'Kelsal!'

Kelsal turned cold with surprise. The boatswain dropped the child, who, despite the shock of finding that water had hardened into wood, or because of it, bounced on to all fours and scrambled through the boatswain's bow-legs and across the deck, where he was hurriedly helped to his feet and pulled into the group of slaves. The second mate eased the girl on to the deck as if lowering her into a bath that might be too hot. She looked at him quickly and ran to Mintah. Mintah held on to her for a moment then nudged her towards the queue. Kelsal's gag was around Mintah's neck. Some of the crew saw it and with wry smiles speculated that Kelsal had given it to her. Mintah's forehead was printed with fine wavery lines. A little blood flecked her mouth, nose and one ear. She stared at Kelsal. Not with any challenge or defiance. It was just a placid look as though they held something in common or had some private understanding which a look as easy as hers would communicate. Kelsal returned her stare. His eyes narrowed and trembled, perhaps against the wind and rain. Did Mintah look changed? She was the woman he had beaten earlier. He had done that. And for good reason. His name was not to be used in this way by a slave. She had been warned, beaten, chained, gagged and here she was again, as impudent with his name as before. She was a fine specimen, would fetch a good price in Jamaica, but he couldn't countenance her another moment on this ship.

'Who unchained her?' Kelsal turned to the crew near him.

The second mate cleared his throat. 'To feed her, like the rest.'

Kelsal wagged his finger in her face. 'That is the last time you call my name.'

Mintah spoke to him rapidly. Whatever she was saying to his face had the effect of rearranging his usual expression. First the furrows between his eyebrows disappeared and his lips parted over his teeth. Then the skin assembled again like an elastic that had been stretched and snapped back to its original shape. His lips pursed once more. But both furrowed skin and lips were made to look worse than before – more grossly furrowed, more tightly pursed – by the temporary alteration. For a while Kelsal seemed to be in pain. He drew a deep breath. He looked at the captain.

'With your permission, Captain?'

The captain nodded his assent and made a rapid, reluctant stroke in his ledger. She is not sick, he thought, though she is enough of a nuisance to cause trouble on this ship. His honest ledger had a stroke for Mintah. He recorded her among the sick and infirm whose presence on the *Zong* jeopardised the health and safety of everyone else. Their judicious disposal as damaged stock would preserve the rest and merit a claim for their loss against the underwriters. Insolence was a sickness. Stubbornness too. Behaviour liable to fuel discontent and promote an insurrection among the slaves was the worst sickness of all. Even his mind, untrained in legal matters, could comprehend this easily, could argue it with facility in a court under English law, if the need ever arose. He could foresee no such need.

'Help me here, Boatswain, Second Mate.'

'Certainly, Mr Kelsal.'

They advanced on Mintah, grabbed her. She kicked,

punched, bit and screamed at them. She was knocked to the deck and lifted by the three crewmen and rushed to the net. A couple of men hurled their bowls at Kelsal and the others and ran to intervene, but the captain's whip across one of their faces brought one to his knees and the other was chopped with a cutlass on his arm so severely that the cutlass stuck in his bone. The crew advanced and beat a few of the slaves indiscriminately to settle them. One of them on lookout in the station above the quarterdeck jumped down and rushed to help. Two others at the cannon followed suit, club and cutlass held high. Kelsal, the boatswain and the second mate could not get Mintah's arms and legs to release them. Her body was through the gap and over the side, but she clung to various parts of the men. They pulled at her hands and feet, and first the left leg then the right disappeared with her body over the side, then her left arm and her right, the hand still gripping a clump of Kelsal's long auburn hair, and then Mintah was gone.

There were screams and shouts from the slaves. Many of the adults emptied their bowls on the deck or simply threw them at the crew. Cutlasses and clubs were used to cut and beat the men and women singled out as the main culprits. The leg irons and fetters made it hard to dodge a blow. Some children crouched down to make themselves inconspicuous; some huddled together afraid to touch their food. The little girl cried into her bowl of porridge and an adult coaxed her to eat. She turned her head away from the proffered spoon. Kelsal looked around, ran his hand delicately over his head, thanked the two men for their assistance and returned to his station beside the captain.

'She didn't look sick to me, Kelsal.' He chuckled to

himself as he waved his ledger at Kelsal and buried it under his cloak.

'Sorry, Captain, my mistake. Shall I look over the side for her?' Kelsal tipped his head to starboard towards the hole in the net.

The two were smiling broadly at each other.

'Got your hair fixed too, I see.'

'Can't find a good barber anywhere these days, Captain.' Kelsal smoothed his hair.

The girl stared at her bowl. Rain covered the porridge like a lavish condiment. Eat, the adult begged, eat for Mintah, so you can grow big, beautiful and strong like her. The child looked up at the adult, wished it was Mintah holding that spoon. But she had seen Mintah flung into the big water, from which no one ever returned. Knowing death had taken Mintah and so would soon take her too, she decided not to feel hunger any more, not to feel anything. To banish hunger in her wait for death to come. She opened her mouth. Closed her eyes. Shut out the wind and the rain. Swallowed the gruel.

Chapter Three

MINTAH'S FIRST IMPRESSION of the high sea was that it was cold and lighter through her fingers and around her skin than it appeared. The sea had the strength of the wind but with more body. Rain welded the sea to the sky. Rain tendrilled her face. Ribbons of water joined to the sea, hauled the sea up, siphoned off sea water for the bloated clouds overhead. Mintah revolved in the current and saw how the rain reversed its flow and became the sea falling upwards, emptying into the sky, billowing the cloud vats that lowered as they gained in volume. Her lungs burned for air. Just as the sea fell upwards, so it was possible to breathe sea water; her mind told her this was so.

When the sea was seen by her for the very first time the tide was out. Water resembled glass. No, rough and hewn wood some ingenious carpenter had planed. So that all the bulbs, glitches and curves dissolved into wood curls to leave it in this state of flatness and calm. From the promontory where she had stood and intertwined fingers just above the eyebrows into a hood against the glare, she had felt with a few steps she could walk on this fashioned wood all the way to the straight line where it ran out and the sky seemed pegged to the ground and light became extinct and an edge she might fall off presented itself. Had she been afraid of the idea? The sea that day had looked inviting. Hadn't she been her father's assistant, a carpenter, wood-carver, wood-engraver? It seemed the sea was to be her first independent project. To be faced without the constant advice over her shoulder and the gentle pressure of a father and teacher's hand at her elbow to guide her plane and chisel. Alone, she could move in on that sea and shape it according to her dreams into forms not seen before and the sea would accommodate her along with all those dreams for as long as she drew breath.

But the tide had been out showing only one side of the sea. Its good side. A sea on its best behaviour: quelled, tamed, untroubled, recumbent. Its other side, the one at war with all the world, including itself, she'd felt before seeing, from below deck. And when she had seen it rough, for the first time, above deck, she'd fallen to her knees surrounded by a tall, wind-blown forest of unplaned, tempestuous wood. She'd crumpled to the deck, fainted. A knot in her chest had been pulled tighter and tighter by the sight of this awakened sea, higher than all the trees she'd known, thick as a wall of tree trunks and moving, marching towards her and over the line of the horizon she had been certain before then that nothing could cross without dying.

Now in the thick of that forest, among its branches, vines and leaves, she believed she was not suffocating, nor tangled up by it, but able to breathe. Mintah parted her lips and inhaled. She breathed the sea. Her body, she fancied, might stretch now, her bones soften and become bendable, until she too reached from sea to sky and was hauled up out of it, over the ship, and deposited in cloud.

She choked on salt and raised her head towards cloud. Wind whipped up the sea and poured it on her head. She threw her arms forward to swim, and hit wood. Opened her eyes and saw the ship's hull passing close by, some giant sea creature whose bulk was submerged, so close she could see that it was barnacled and mossy and sprouted what looked to her salted eyes like vines. She stretched out her arm and grabbed at the wood. It was rough and spurned her clutches. The grain was there but buried. Or else had detached itself from the wood, dissociated itself from it by twisting itself into a plait and dangling off the wood. She grabbed at the plaited grain and held on to it, stopped swimming and found she was being dragged along with the ship. She pulled herself close to the hull and saw the rope she clung to stretching up to an air vent where several ropes dangled off boats used to supply the ship when anchored offshore and, higher up, to rigging that led up the side. She glanced back at the ship's wake several feet away and saw fins in the water criss-crossing the white spume. Fins zoomed towards her, slicing the water and growing as they approached. The ship arrowed ahead, the sea leapt and swayed, wind thrust and parried, rain curlicued and peppered her face, clouds boiled and floated. Her head spun. The fins moved fastest of all as if on a mission, but Mintah felt adrift. The fins wanted her. Their speed and purpose was inspired by her. A minuscule impulse instructed her it would be best, under the circumstances, to surrender to those fins. She blinked rapidly to clear her eyes and banish that thought. A few feet from her, the nearest fin dived out of view. Mintah pulled her body from the sea and drew her legs up into the air. She swung against the hull with the sway of the ship, searched with her toes for a grip and managed to support her weight a little by sticking her toenails into a small gap between two caulked boards whose oakum had worked loose. Then she straightened, suppressed an urge to cough and peered upwards through the ribbons of rain and climbed. Her view was obliterated by the rain. She reached an air vent. Other ropes hung from the boats higher up. Her arms pulled her up about eighteen inches while her feet steadied her and held her position by clutching the rope between the big first toes and second toes, then her arms would pull again and draw her up a little more and again her toes would search for and find the rope and grip it and anchor her. At last she gained the closest boat and rolled into it. Her body burned with the effort.

The boat was full of rain. She drank the water and diluted the sea she'd swallowed. She lay in the boat and floated. Once her breathing was under control and her arms pained her less she resumed her climb. Her arms and legs ached. Breathing as hard as she could did nothing to ameliorate the searing inside. The thought of letting go and falling back into the sea and not moving a muscle ever again, so that there would be no aches and fires and she would feel bodiless and free, loomed in her head. But she could feel the wood she cherished against her body, drawing her upwards and promising safety at any moment, an end to the blistering and scorching soon. The rain felt sharp. Each drop was a needle pelted at her. Wind burned her; a huge flame that sidled up to her, that she shrank to avoid but was surrounded by. The ship's hull scraped her skin. 'Let go, Mintah!' She heard the voice above the wind and the rain and the sea, above all the flames, inside her body and out. Her hands gripped the rope but she felt nothing. A stranger's hand. She glanced down at her legs and feet, clutching the rope. They too seemed numb. Someone else's legs and feet.

54

What ignited, if not her body? Whose body burned? The thought stopped her and she clung to the rope without trying even to hold on to it. To fall back into the sea, she knew she had merely to think the thought, picture the fall and those stranger's hands and feet that kept her in pain would release her. 'Let go!' A large porthole expelled something that was charred. A branding of flesh but not hers. Mintah breathed through her nose. The smell filled her head. It fumigated her mind, driving out the voice that had urged her to fall back into the sea. Mintah thrust her legs into the porthole and drew her body in. She released the rope, one hand at a time, and grabbed the porthole. Then she climbed into what she recognised right away as the kitchen because of that smell of incinerated food. She fell into the gloomy apothecary-like den, too weak to stand. She lay on her back and breathed, loving the smell of that burning food, all the while worrying that someone would walk in and grab her and this time she would be too weak to even look at them as they flung her back overboard. Not now, she thought. Not after all I've done. She rolled on to her stomach, pushed herself upright and, holding a chair, pulled herself into it and rested a little, before taking a few unsteady steps to a pot on the stove. She examined the cook's bubbling concoction intended for unsuspecting stomachs. Beef stewing beyond recognition. Plate in hand, Mintah spooned the gravy and thought it wiser not to taste it before serving herself. She decided to approach it not as food for the palate, but as sustenance for the body. By this trick of reasoning she was able to fill her plate and begin to find her way to a deeper, darker, more remote section of the ship. As she picked through the dark, growing accustomed to the ship's sway, she placed bits of the stew in her mouth.

The storeroom was less than half full. Mintah clambered over bags of rice, yams, potatoes, she sidled around barrels of water, barrels of palm oil, cask upon cask of malt liquor, bushels of salt, stacked chests of corn, circumnavigated with excess care pounds of malaguetta pepper, puncheons of dried beef, hundredweights of flour, hundredweights of biscuits, resisted the temptation of wine barrels, fingered for their texture the bags of beans and deliberately sniffed at bags of oatmeal. Everything in the room was raw or dried, yet all had a more pleasant aroma and feel than the food she had eaten over the last ten weeks. Still, she thought it prudent to clean her plate, found a water barrel and drank and chose a corner farthest from the door to lie down and think.

'I am alive,' she said aloud to herself. An involuntary chuckle erupted from her. Her hand came up to her forehead. The wood-grain that was branded there had been erased and the smoothness of her skin restored. She laughed out loud. Placed her hand over her mouth. Her body shook with laughter. She could not stop. She brought her knees up and rolled on to her side and clutched her stomach which ached with a sweetness she hadn't known for months. Her eyes streamed. She slapped the bags of supplies that surrounded her, hugged her stomach, covered her mouth, wished she had more hands to do all the things she wanted to do as she laughed. And the involuntary paroxysm gradually abated leaving her feeling light and giddy and sleepy.

She slipped into sleep without any time to consider the wisdom of it. Her body demanded it. But her mind, in its ceaseless deliberations, simply swapped the ship for land. Mintah running behind her mother leaving her father standing, chisel in hand, at the gate of their compound after her parents had argued about gods. After the missionaries were welcomed among her people, their work had come to this: choose between gods. Her father was not convinced by the missionaries' insistence that one deity was responsible for everything he saw in the world. Any single thing in all its permutations and manifestations was thought by his people enough of a complexity for one god to worry about. Take wood, for instance. One god would have to devote all his time and energy to keeping up with what wood does, never mind what he, armed with his chisel, did with it. Other gods kept abreast of other things, and all things worked together because the gods cooperated.

Her mother retorted that this single god watched over the entire world and made it all and that praising him must preclude sacrifices, drums and dancing and offer instead quiet and still reflection and a new set of rules and regulations aimed at improving everyone. The argument ran for days and patience ran out on both sides. Then they stopped talking to each other and her father began to curse the day the missionaries set foot in their town and her mother shouted at him for saying nasty things about the holy men.

When it was time for the missionaries to leave for the coast Mintah's mother and a small group decided to follow. Her father refused to uproot. He said he had too much he could not bear to part with. He said if she stayed he would reconsider his position about this one god as long as he could carry on his work with wood and praise the wood-god. Her mother said no. One god or nothing; one god made the world, not a committee of gods.

Mintah ran to keep up with her mother and looked back at her father standing by the gate leading into their compound with his chisel which he raised in a gesture that was either a goodbye wave or a beckoning to her to come back.

Her mother's hand had reached down then and taken hers and they carried on fast, Mintah trotting to keep up, until they caught the others and were greeted with smiles and kind words. Then they slowed down and Mintah turned to see if her father had followed them, but there was only the empty track, her father was gone, their compound and the town gone too.

'Are you dead?' Mintah woke to the voice and her shoulders being shaken. She did not remember falling asleep. Where am I? she wondered. A picture of a ship gathered into focus and loomed, suspended in a bright light. Not the ship she knew. This ship seemed to fly in light and air.

'Are you dead?' Her shoulders rattled again. Who is speaking to me? she asked herself. The ship leaned in the wind and a deluge of men, women, children, whips, chains, cutlasses, guns, howls and screams made her sit bolt upright. A young man stood over her holding a machete next to his head. His face was pale, freckled naturally or by the sun she couldn't tell, with large blue eyes that looked more afraid than angry.

'Didn't they throw you over the side?'

'Yes.'

'Then you must be a witch.'

She paused, and looked up at his frightened face. 'How old are you?'

'Old enough.'

'What are you doing here?'

'I work here.'

'Who are you? The cook's assistant?'

'Look, let me ask the questions.'

'All right, ask.'

58

'And don't start giving me orders, like Cook. I come down here to get something, I forget what, and find you here.'

Mintah knew this young man. His mind was simple. He was beaten for every mistake he made. The cook treated him with a disdain only a little less marked than that reserved for slaves.

'What did I come down here for?' He looked around him, baffled. 'See what you gone and done. Made me forget. Now Cook will beat me.'

He sat down with his head on his knees. Mintah edged closer to him. She thought about touching the blond hair sweeping down the sides of his face, if only to look more closely at the expression there.

'I'll help you remember.'

'What you going to do, read Cook's mind from in here?'

'No, read yours.'

The young man stopped worrying and looked at her. He raised his machete beside his head.

'Don't worry, this won't hurt.' Mintah smiled. 'Now why are you carrying a machete?'

'I don't know.'

'Did you have to cut something with it?'

'Yes, I had to cut something for Cook.'

She couldn't be sure, but he did seem to be playing along with her.

'So what is there in this room that needs to be chopped?'

They began to search in the bags. Mintah held up a handful of rice.

'Rice! You don't cut rice with a machete. Even I know that.'

They got to the beans. He dipped his palm in, held it up

and shook his head and laughed. Mintah shrugged off the thought that so far in their exchange it was she not he who was the foolish one. She saw the yams and ignored them until he came to them and held one up triumphantly.

'Yams! A piece of yam, Cook said, bigger than a nigger's head but not as big as a white man's.'

Mintah brought her hand up to her mouth.

'What? Not yam?' He put the yam down, dejected. But there was a mischievous sparkle in his eyes.

'Yes, yam. Cut it and go before he comes looking for you.'

He chopped a yam in two with one swing of his machete. Mintah's eyes widened.

'I'm good in the kitchen, with knives and things like that.'

'I can see. Don't tell anyone I'm here. Let it be our secret.'

The young man nodded and smiled and backed away a few steps.

'And come and see me soon.'

'Yes.' At the door, he paused and said her name.

'You know my name?'

'All the slaves are saying your name.'

'What's yours?'

But he was already out the door and had closed it behind him.

Mintah paced around the supplies. Any moment she expected to hear footsteps running to apprehend her. She had to find another place. But where? Anywhere, was all she could come up with. She lifted the door handle and pulled. Locked. She tugged at it repeatedly. How could it be locked? She ran back to her place at the back of the storeroom, behind the supplies, and sat down. Mintah resolved that when they came for her she would face them and fight them as she had done before and she would say that name like the curse it was. If she had to face the sea a second time so be it.

Land. If only she was on land. She could run in one direction away from these people and hide. There would be no limit to the number of hiding places. This ship was nowhere. The grain in its wood offered small comforts. She was tired of the threat of the sea. It appalled her that she could be in the middle of nowhere for weeks at a time, surrounded by sea and a distant horizon promising more sea. How could she even think she was alive in this situation? She hadn't seen a tree, bush, flower, bird, insect or animal in three months. Water promised nothing. A life on water was no life to live, just an in-between life, a suspended life, a life in abeyance, until land presented itself and enabled that life to resume.

What had she left behind, in her life on land? A mission, a mother. Before that a father, a chisel. Before that little things. Short time-frames of things with no connection, stored haphazardly inside. Disparate supplies lumped together in a room to support a balanced diet. A diet of recall. And a diet of promises. She raided their store-room periodically to sustain her, and far from being emptied by her raids she found she was simply retrieving the same things time and again from that room and they yielded nothing new and had now ceased to offer comfort. Had now become a source of agitation to her. For she wanted to live, to get beyond a dependence on what had happened in an increasingly distant past, and to accrue newer moments, better things, for her future comfort.

Mintah heard a key clang into a lock. She held her breath. Iron rubbed iron and turned against wood and the door to the storeroom opened. Her heart bucked and kicked as if to demolish the wall of her chest. She braced her body against the wall and looked at a spot unblink-ingly, listening with her eyes. Footsteps approached her hiding place. Mintah stared at the cook's assistant and he returned her gaze. They spoke simultaneously.

'Why did you lock the door?'

'How did you get in here?'

Mintah waited for him to speak while he waited for her.

'You must speak first.'

'The door was open.'

'I thought that's what you'd say.'

He turned and walked out. She heard him fiddling with the key in the lock and she heard him test the handle to make sure he had had success.

'But what's your name?' She didn't mean to shout. More key in lock noises and he appeared holding the key on a string around his neck.

'Simon.'

He exited and repeated the key and lock routine. Then everything quietened, except for the wind, rain and sea. Mintah scraped her back down the wall until she came to a sitting position and exhaled loudly. She listened to her heart settle to its usual activity and to her breathing which deepened and evened out. All this room was hers. She could stretch, kick, turn over, spin, breathe and dance, unobstructed, without injuring someone pushed up against her on all sides.

Where had she had such privacy before? Nowhere she could think of. Not at home, where she shared a space used for meals and conversation by lying on a grass mat in a corner that doubled as a seat during the day. Nor at the mission, where all the children slept in a long wooden hut on mats that had to be tidied into a corner in the morning for Bible lessons. This was her first time alone in a wooden room. And where was she? Not in a place where she could savour it. Not in any place. On water. On a geography that constantly rearranged itself as if to dupe the traveller, or keep its secrets from the explorer by constantly redrawing its maps.

The walk away from her father to the coast with her mother and the missionaries had taken her over a plain with tall grass only her head bobbed above, across streams with stone steps or broad felled trees, so broad she was able to walk next to her mother, above a waterfall and above the world as they walked through its mists and its thunder, down into forests where the sun was filtered green and in a clearing where the sun seemed as solid as a tree trunk and the sounds of the forests echoed or were clamorous. And they had seen all the animals described by the old people in stories at night by the fire, had heard all their sounds, elephants, giraffes, antlered deer, that looked and sounded exactly as mimicked by those old men and women. All were on a map that was fixed, one she was sure she could find again. If she lived.

But this sea could never be found. There was no particular place on or in it to find. It mimicked peaks and valleys for brief spells. And sometimes the animals on the plains or in the forests were there in the sea breezes. And the sun on a clear day, uninterrupted by cloud or a breeze or rain, planted itself in the sea as immovable as a thick forest.

Wood might shape these things for her one day. A chisel and wood, in a wooden room just for her. Not a room to hide in and disappear but one for work. In it she would please the god of wood with her arrangements of wood-grain. The room would fill with wood-shavings and their perfume. Objects made by her would clutter it, like these supplies, but there would always be room for more objects. She would build this room wherever she ended up with this ship. And the land she left behind, against her will, would take shape in this room, and sooner or later the room would become that land. And she would have lost nothing.

God, the God who presides over everything, who makes all other gods irrelevant, and to whom everyone is answerable, above husbands, wives, above parents, above brother, lover and sister, the God she associated with the coast, figured in her prayers. Mintah asked for forgiveness. For what she did to deserve this fate. For her continued loyalty to traditional gods. Not even gods, just one god, that of wood, and sometimes the god of fertility. She kneeled into the ship's sea-induced camber with her palms clasped and fingers knitted and begged to God. Her final request was for life on land. She begged God to spare her and the rest of her people from a death by drowning. If she got to land, whatever life she had to lead there, she promised she would serve Him to the end of her days.

She lay on her right side with her back against a bag of rice that returned a back's shape. This prompted a last thought for her companions, stacked like books on shelves below. She would lie still for them. More still than the night spread evenly outside. Not turn more than necessary, or sprawl her arms and legs, or stretch too much, for them. 'God,' she begged, 'let me sleep in peace. I do not deserve Your mercy but let me sleep.'

Where did sleep come from? It ascended from the sea and carried her off, even as her mind quarrelled with everything in it, even as she prayed as part of that quarrel. Her brow may have felt the cool shadow of sleep settle and iron out the furrows there. Yet she did not. Her mind may have seen the shadow too late to do anything but fall silent. For suddenly she was worrying about everything and feeling every ache in her body, and as suddenly she felt nothing, not even the rice bag of another's back, nothing but emptiness, which for her was peace, was sleep. She had rolled on to her stomach, her head cradled in one arm, the other hand by her side, one knee bent, the other straight, as she had always slept on land. Her sleep was deep and dreamless.

Chapter Four

T HE DAY HAD lodged itself between the shoulders of the *Zong*'s entire crew. It ached there. They felt drained of their blood to feed that ache. Morning had been succeeded by evening, not according to the orchestrations of light since cloud and rain had kept it sequestered in the heavens, but by an accumulation of this ache in them. Captain Cunningham added the day's strokes in his ledger, the sick strokes as he called them, in the company of his first and second mates and his boatswain, invited into his cabin out of the darkness and rain.

'Fifty-four!'

The boatswain marvelled at this statistic produced by their collective labours. But Kelsal and the second mate seemed less than enthusiastic.

'I think we have earned ourselves a generous brandy.'

'Hear! Hear!' all three agreed with the captain.

He decanted the amber distillation into their cups, poured for himself last and they drank to each other's health and a healthy profit for their recent endeavours. They threw their heads back and smacked their lips or exhaled loudly. The boatswain stamped his right heel and might have whinnied like a happy stallion had he not been in the captain's company. A happy, alcohol-induced complicity united the four men. Nothing was said. They faced each other in a tight circle and sipped their cups. Captain Cunningham punctured the silence. 'Nearly halfway there I would say, wouldn't you, Kelsal?'

Kelsal jerked to attention then settled back into the stoop in his shoulders which worsened with his frown.

'Only halfway?'

He looked at his second mate, who nodded his encouragement. But the boatswain avoided Kelsal's eyes and kept his gaze on the captain. The captain took this as his cue to reply.

'We are availing ourselves of a decent profit margin.'

'But there aren't that many sick.'

Again Kelsal looked at his second mate, who nodded as before.

'From your behaviour this afternoon, Kelsal, one would not believe that you view this whole enterprise with distaste. That female was not infirm by any stretch of the imagination, yet here she lies, a sick stroke in this honest book. How are we to make up her value? How else than by a claim for her, and for every other debilitated piece of stock on this ship!'

Captain Cunningham banged his ledger. Kelsal watched the ledger and the hand resting on it, unable to avert his eyes and risk meeting the captain's and the boatswain's resentful looks. He understood that the captain's patience was wearing thin with what seemed like indecision on his, Kelsal's, part. But the feeling he had inside would not leave him. The female had brought it on by a mere calling of his name. And with each slave disposed of, the churning sensation in his stomach had intensified. He thought she was the cause and therefore her disposal would end it. The opposite was the case. He ate and vomited. Now this brandy burning inside, that he supposed a good cure, was beginning to feel as though he had consumed a brimful cup of sour milk.

'Excuse me, Captain, Second Mate, Boatswain.'

He rushed out of the cabin, through the quarterdeck door into the early evening rain and barely made it to the side, where he voided the contents of his stomach, watched by some of the crew, one or two of whom cheered, thinking him drunk and the night so young.

'What's the matter with that man? Is he losing his stomach for the job?' The boatswain was seeking the captain's approval and got it.

'It would appear so, Boatswain.'

The second mate cut his eyes at the boatswain and piped up in Kelsal's defence.

'Mr Kelsal was marooned on the coast for a considerable spell, nearly a year, and spent time with the natives. He lived among them. Does that not entitle him to a certain tender feeling for them?'

The boatswain avoided the second mate's glare and looked to the captain for an answer. Captain Cunningham shook his head as he spoke.

'Doubtless Kelsal knows these slaves better than all of us put together. With his knowledge he should handle them with more expertise, not less; more stomach, not less.'

The boatswain laughed and clinked cups with the captain, but the second mate stared down at his feet.

Kelsal ducked into the cabin again.

'Sorry, gentlemen, I seem to have got a gripe of the stomach.'

The boatswain glanced furtively at the captain. Both smirked.

'If you prefer, First Mate, I can assign tomorrow's

68

disposal of another parcel of cargo to Second Mate, or Boatswain.'

'I would view that as the captain's lack of confidence in me, sir.'

'You're a good, reliable man, Kelsal, don't let me down.'

'No, Captain.'

'We stand to gain tremendously from this venture, providing we are resolute. Right, gentlemen?'

'Aye, aye, Captain!'

They filed out of his cabin and dispersed. Walking to compensate for the ship's lean, each catapulted himself from one fixed object to another in quick, awkward steps, clutching at each station momentarily to recover his balance, then hurtling forward again. All three did indeed appear under the influence of the captain's brandy. But their clear commands to the crew indicated otherwise. Tasks were split between checking the cordage, the eight sails, the guns and ammunition, the rigging, and clearing the deck of discarded bowls and spoons and the cook's servings of spilled and, in many cases, deliberately dumped porridge, that made the deck resemble a cow pasture.

Rain eased to a drizzle as if its progress were slowed by the thickened dark. Captain Cunningham decided to pace the deck for exercise and for a little reflection. His presence on deck always instilled in his men a sense of virtuous industry, no lewd talk and an air of business. In actuality, they worked with half an eye on the captain, only half-attending to what they knew as second nature. Their partial focus on their tasks, feeling their way along almost, created the inverse impression that they were concentrating, but concentration inappropriate to the mundane work they were engaged in. How could the captain know he was being scrutinised when the fashion of it was so oblique? Or that every second of his presence on deck was a source of resentment because it enforced an undue vigilance in his crew? Perhaps he knew that the territory of his captaincy had delineations such as these in it that he could do nothing about, would wish, in fact, to do nothing about, and positively relied upon, for his effectiveness as captain. Maybe that was precisely why he chose to walk at this time, under these insalubrious conditions, on deck.

All his working life he had been in the trade. He began with a scrubbing brush and a bucket of vinegar water and a bar of soap and faced the vast expanse of a dirty deck and got on his knees and scrubbed. A topsail's rigging had, on more than one occasion in his early years, been untangled by him in a storm or the sail itself unfurled by his hand, climbing the rigging with trembling legs and praying not to fall with each step. Each rank he had ascended through still lived in him. Each decision he came to as captain relied on a careful balancing of opinions expressed by these differing selves. Years ago when he was a second mate, he practised thinking as a first mate in order to learn the rudiments of that job and anticipate its demands. Now he was captain and had to think ahead of his captaincy to the next role up, that of investor.

Everything hinged on him. The investors would blame him for any loss of stock if those losses dented their profits. His next captaincy hinged, not on his life's experience in this abominable but necessary trade, as he often referred to it, but on his last performance. And that performance was measured solely by profit yielded. The mathematics, performed in some coffee house or other in the Strand, was simple. Out here, at sea, those simple additions and subtractions, multiplications and long divisions were another matter altogether.

If the sick, in their present numbers, survived until the ship limped into Jamaican waters, they would fetch a pittance at auction in their condition. He would make too little to fill the converted hold with sugar for the trip to Liverpool. There would be ample excuses to offer, to be sure – dysentery, the flux, fever, smallpox – but the backers in their fine linens would wave him from them with a flap of their embroidered, scented handkerchiefs, and strut away, damning the day he was born and the moment they entrusted him with their investment.

Did his life depend on it? No. With a little application he could turn his mind to other means of procuring a living. But the trade was all he knew, he couldn't change at this advanced stage in his life. If the profits were big he would consider making this voyage his last. His mind had already manufactured his retirement: land-locked in his native Lancashire, with his pipe, his head bare, his slippered feet up on a stool, facing a grate that never smouldered, with a brandy fuming in a glass near at hand.

His company would be hand-picked, no one on this ship. Maybe Kelsal before his recent moodiness. Certainly not his obsequious boatswain. The second mate if a couple of others could be found to offset his obvious lack of intellect. A wife would be useful. She'd warm his bed and scratch those itches high up and near the middle of his back that necessitated his resorting to door frames. With his means he could get the pick of the bunch.

All these years he'd been too busy to marry. He had left sweethearts who'd forgotten him after nearly a year away. Who could blame them? They'd told him, blunt to his face, that they thought he had died or that they'd had a change of heart or just plain settled for a man who was around on those long winter nights when a bed can seem as big as the sea and as lonely.

He had offered a defence that had sounded lame even to his own sympathetic ears: that his letters home, though punctuated by long intervals of unavoidable silence, nevertheless expressed his continuing interest in his lovers; that delays and other unforeseen circumstances were a footnote to every voyage, and the rumours, always in parentheses (constant false rumours about such and such's death or desertion spread in the broadsheets and in England's taverns and coffee houses) were insufficient grounds for consigning him to the grave.

Captain Cunningham thought about his judges at home, pronouncing on him. They all seemed to know what went on at sea. Everyone purported to be an expert. Yet few would ever come to view the sea as companionable. Would ever know how a man could actually think at sea. When a man had ploughed the sea as long as he had he soon viewed it as an adversary, and wondered, as he had pondered every day at sea, if he was worthy to face it.

All his actions thus far, prior to their execution, had been justified to God. A qualification for doing anything had always been 'How would this look in the eyes of God?' He asked himself this searching question over the issue of what to do with the mounting sick among his holdings on the *Zong* before he had reached his decision. Under English law it was stated that every slave bought and sold in the trade was categorised as stock. As such, an owner could do with his stock whatever he pleased. Certain practices had evolved to keep within that law, and within the confines of boundaries governing the conduct of Christians engaged in the trade. God's largesse was not intended to be conferred on every life form that crawled over the globe, though every life form would earn a place in Paradise by virtue of the fact of its innocent existence on earth. Humanity's place was special, privileged. These privileges were earned by the faculty of language and by harnessing the world's resources to the betterment of mankind. How could they be reasonably extended to the African who was so obviously below the rest of humanity? To do so would be to squander and cheapen the very notion of godhead conferred on a newborn as his birthright and validated by him through virtuous Christian living. These subtle gradations were lost on the African. And whilst it was desirable to be good to them as one would be just and equitable with any stock, they were not fully formed *Homo sapiens*. Heaven was not theirs through salvation or prayer or baptism, and if they were incapacitated through illness it would be a merciful owner indeed who decided to curtail their suffering through their speedy disposal.

'Good night, gentlemen.' He intended this greeting for all hands in the vicinity of his cabin.

'Good night to you, Captain Cunningham,' the crew responded, from all parts of the main and the quarter-deck. Their animation at the prospect of his departure was thinly veiled, compared to the muted slowness with which they had faced their drudgery during his peram-bulation.

Captain Cunningham knew this. He also knew it would not be prudent to remain on deck any longer, nor to reappear that evening. He would have to rely on his officers to maintain civility among the lower ranks during his absence. They would have to be his eyes and his ears. After all, he was only human. He could not be in two places at once. In his absence something of his discipline, he hoped, would remain alive in the minds of his crew.

73

Was this wishful thinking on his part? He thought not. Their minds and inclinations were familiar territory to him. An enclosed few acres rather than a continent. Neither held any surprises for him. Not like the sea – shifty, ambiguous, unfathomable.

The moment the captain vanished into his cabin the second mate and the boatswain descended into the female slaves' partition armed with loaves of bread and chunks of cheese, and announced to any takers what they stood to gain by accompanying them and communicated their intent by waving the provisions around and beckoning to the women to follow. Most of the women were hungry and exhausted, but the ones with children to feed or who felt too hungry to sleep were tempted. What was required of them? A few minutes with these men for bread and cheese. Not the cook's pulped beans, or the small helping of rice mixed with yam or, if they were lucky, a thin strip of dried beef, but bread reserved for the captain and officers. And if they refused they would be taken by force anyway. The women knew all this when they gave their consent for bread and cheese.

Soon other sailors appeared with other or similar inducements: rum, biscuits, a slice of lemon or lime, bits of beef, even a trinket or two. But trinkets were trouble because someone would want to take them, and there was always someone willing to fight for them. A refusal would lead to a beating, to being singled out for special hardships and abuse. And here no one wanted to be singled out for anything since it was rarely a good thing that would come that person's way from the crew.

The second mate and the boatswain took their women below to the two cabins (really one small cabin divided by a partition) where they slept, but their subordinates simply found a dark corner on the deck in which to carry out their transactions. Where rum was involved their bullying and lewd directives to the women had to be hushed and suppressed by more sober crewmen. A woman knew she risked being bribed by one man and then set upon by others immediately afterwards once she left the relative safety of the women's quarters. Only a woman of superb pride would refuse bread and cheese when hungry, and there were some. But a refusal carried with it the risk of serious personal harm if the crew then ganged together to take what they could not get by asking and what in any case they saw as rightfully theirs.

The men chained hand and foot in pairs in their section heard all this and sometimes were beneficiaries of the proceeds. A piece of bread and cheese was handed to them in the dark and they accepted it with thanks and ate it. If a few found it hard to swallow knowing how it was earned, it was not out of resentment for the woman, who had to do what she did for reasons they all knew, but because they were choked with anger at the men who could do such a thing to captive women. They wanted to break their chains and rush on to the deck and strangle those men and then throw them into the sea. One man reproached the women for not being like Mintah, for not having an ounce of her dignity and pride. A woman's voice replied that dignity and pride made an awful diet and, as witnessed by them all, resulted in a shortened life, a good life thrown away. Dignity and pride, the voice continued, taught the children how to die young, when they needed to learn how to live in a world no one had dreamed could ever be.

The women would return to the slave hold and wriggle into a space between other women. They would grab what sleep they could. Semen from the crew would seep from them on to the deck; children were at various stages of gestation in their wombs. Or wombs unable to function in these conditions would be the recipients of some disease or other. Wombs in abeyance; emptied of their fecundity. Amnesiacal wombs, forgetting to bleed, forgetting their function. Wombs that declared everything that had happened to this body had to end there. There would be no inheritance from these wombs.

If the women cried because of what was done to them against their will, it would have to be silently, though every shudder or whimper would doubtless be detected by a neighbour. Below decks tears were commonplace. What would the neighbour do? Silence those tears. They were contagious. That shudder, if allowed to continue, would have spread through the hold and awakened everyone and taken them all over. Then the sleep so badly needed would have fled those confines, and some bodies might have been broken beyond repair, broken by their susceptibility to tears once and for all time. So those women were cursed under the breath, elbowed, ordered to be silent and cease fidgeting. Rarely, a hand would land softly on a trembling shoulder and pat it, or a head would be patted and soothing words uttered.

On their capture the women had thought they were slaves destined to be eaten. Then they had revised this to forced labour. After these nights they thought of themselves as slaves, as someone who was meant to be no one. There was no room for dignity or pride, not in any recognisable form. Both had been buried in the deep sea of who they were before their capture. They shared a recurring dream in which dignity and pride were resurrected from those depths, salvaged and restored.

Mintah had demonstrated to them what *not* to do. Do not raise your voice to these people. Do not look them in the eye. Do not lift the chin off the chest since to show the soft space of the neck and windpipe is to risk attack. Do not call their name in vain or for any reason unless they explicitly request it. Do not cross them with disobedience, they will attack. Do not tell them no, they never take no for an answer, they believe no means yes, they will get what they want in the end. Do not tell them anything about yourself, they will use it against you and all your kind. Do not trust any of them, they are all the same, seeing you as profit, as fit only to buy and sell, and with nothing else to recommend you. Do not rely on them for anything, they are untrustworthy with everything but money. Do not think they will ever grow to love you; you were purchased by them, therein lies the extent of their praise and the limits of their love. Do not let them throw you into the sea, unless you prefer death to life. Do not let them remember you like Mintah.

Chapter Five

DAWN CLARIFIED IN the rigging, which was one tangled mass in the dark but now revealed itself as an intricate skeleton deliberately pitched against the sky. The morning brought more rain with it and only a meagre crop of light. Night skulked around in thick cloud refusing to budge for the new day. Simon waited at the cook's side for his next assignment. His blond hair was parted neatly down the middle, and instead of being left to fall over the sides of his face it was combed back behind his round, slightly protruding ears. Pots of porridge bubbled on three fires stoked and fanned by Simon. The cook looked irritated and about to lash out at the nearest person.

'Salt.'

Simon handed him the salt, viewing him askance.

'What do you think?'

A steaming spoon was held up by the cook for Simon to taste. This surprised Simon. He reacted slowly then hurried to cut off any insult.

'Well, take the spoon, lad, I'm not going to feed you.'

Simon took it without spilling the gooey mixture, and sucked the end.

'What do you think? A breakfast fit for a slave?'

'Yes, Cook. More than fit.'

'Good. Get the pails then.'

As the rain had not abated, breakfast would be distributed to the slaves in their cramped quarters. A bucket for each group of ten or so to squabble over. Things were going like a dream for Simon this morning. He hadn't been hit once by Cook, nor verbally abused. It felt unusual and pleasant. For this morning at least, Cook was his friend.

'I've got a secret.' Cook did not seem to hear him. He piped up again. 'I said I've got a secret.'

This time the cook paused over one of his pots and looked at Simon as if he were the next ingredient to be added to it.

'Is that so? And what secret would that be, lad?'

'That would be telling, wouldn't it?'

The cook became intrigued with the exchange. A rueful smile played around the left side of his mouth and cheek, unwilling to form properly.

'It can't be much of a secret if you can't tell it.'

'What do you mean?'

'Well, good secrets are worth telling; stupid secrets aren't worth the space in the head devoted to storing them.'

Simon had to pause and think about this for a while. The cook's smile surfaced a little more and spread to the other side of his face, but from his expression it still seemed indecisive about breaking out and declaring itself as a smile.

'You mean if I tell you my secret, then it's a good secret, but if I don't then it's not worthy?'

'In a word, yes!'

Simon weighed this up in his head. A broad smile took

over the cook's face. He held it, savoured it and left off stirring his porridge to witness his victory over Simon.

'No, no. I can't tell.'

Cook's smile dissolved. He reddened in a flash.

'Tell me your stupid secret or I'll give you a hiding!'

'You called it stupid, I'm not telling.'

Cook pulled his spoon from the pot and lashed Simon with it. Simon held up his arms, which collected the blows intended for his head. He screamed with the heat.

'Get out of my sight, you simpleton.'

Simon grabbed two pails, dodged a swipe from the cook, and headed down the ship along a narrow gangway leading to the female section of the slave hold.

'What a waste of breath that boy is.' Cook felt his sense of triumph evaporate. Simon would have to pay for that, he decided, with a few more blows and lashes.

Halfway along the corridor, Simon stopped in his tracks and took a detour to the storeroom. At the door he put down the pails, dried his eyes and fished the key on its string out of his shirt. He practised a smile, fixed it to his face and unlocked the door. Mintah's broad smile greeted his own.

'Good morning, Mintah.'

'And a very good morning to you, Simon.'

'Are you hungry?'

'Yes, I can't wait to try Cook's latest concoction.'

'What do you mean?'

'Goes by the name of porridge.'

He was smiling because she was smiling. He held out a bowl and spoon and told her she could borrow them since he'd already eaten. Mintah held out her hand and touched Simon's arm and gave it three quick strokes. He looked at the place between his elbow and right shoulder for a while after she had withdrawn her hand, as if her hand rubbing his skin had given him a sparkling new set of muscles. Porridge slid reluctantly from the tipped pail and amassed sulkily in the bowl. Mintah took her first mouthful, chewed and gulped it down. She nodded slowly as an opinion about the porridge descended from her head to her mouth.

'Porridge.'

They laughed. Simon hurried out and locked the door behind him. As he marched along the narrow gangway, he found that he could not stop his smile. Mintah made him laugh, Cook made him cry. Mintah was a woman, Cook a man. He decided to feed the women first.

The stench at the entrance to the women's holding area wiped off his smile. He handed over the pails and scooted back to the kitchen, followed by a couple of women who would help to fetch and distribute the porridge.

When he returned to the slave hold a commotion between three crewmen and a group of women blocked his path. The crewmen had a sick woman in their clutches, and as they tugged to remove her, her legs were held by three women pulling her back into the hold. They fended off one crewman's club. There was shouting and cursing and screaming. More of the crew came down the hatch. Other women jumped to the sick woman's defence and pelted porridge, bowls and spoons into the faces of the crew, inviting blows from the clubs on their heads and arms. In the middle of it all the sick woman remained quiet. A final tug by the crew freed her from the women and she was hauled through the hatch and into the morning light and rain.

The second mate clawed porridge from his eyes and shouted to Simon to return those pails of ammunition to the kitchen. Simon retreated. Three more of the crew came down the steps into the gangway and cleared a path with their clubs towards more of the sick. As before two lifted and carried while the third swiped at the women who crowded around them.

Captain Cunningham stood under a canvas shelter, ledger in hand, last night's sleep still crusted in his eyes. He made a stroke as each sick person was borne past him, carried to the side and tossed overboard. As one team ascended to the hatch with a sick slave, a second set descended to apprehend another. The crew took leg irons with them to fetter the sick who were now putting up more of a fight. With the men the operation involved even greater effort since the sick had to be unshackled from the men they were paired off with and newly shackled to be conveyed above deck and over the side.

Kelsal appointed himself identifier of the sick. He roamed the shelves with his stoop and his stare combined into a body and mask donned by death. The slaves recoiled from him as death itself walked up to them and pointed them out as its own. Kelsal was alert. Faces had to be scrutinised, eyes searched for the tell-tale dullness he associated with sickness. One man spat in his face. Kelsal beat the man on the head and, when the man covered his head, about the arms and shoulders, and cursed and ordered his crew to remove the offender. The air was so foul from the overnight effluvia of the chained bodies that Kelsal was forced to retreat for fresh air or risk losing the contents of his stomach yet again.

The second mate requested a break for his men. Kelsal nodded but asked the second mate to wait a moment while he consulted with the captain. Captain Cunningham was irritated, but he could see that the men were breathless and struggling to lift the pieces of stock over the side so he agreed that they should resume after lunch. The ledger was closed and tucked under his arm and he left the deck for the shelter of his cabin.

Kelsal told his crew that the entire slave hold would have to be washed and fumigated. Vinegar diluted in water heated with shot was sloshed on the shelves and women were enlisted to scrub the soiled planks with a metal scraper and wire brushes. To contain the slaves, small areas were washed at a time and the slaves brought above deck in batches of twenty. Those who hadn't eaten were served the porridge that had gone cold and ordered to wash then returned below. This routine continued until the crew stopped for lunch.

A light rain needled the ship throughout all this industry. Though the sky remained grey it was not dark. The wind had died down to an occasional whistling around the decks rather than the previous constant howl. But the seas remained a series of peaks and valleys with only a marginal lengthening in the distances between the two. Many of the male slaves were bruised and bleeding around their ankles and wrists from the endless tugs on their chains as one or other was pulled in the opposite direction by a sudden lurch of the ship. Kelsal thought it prudent to offer them something in the way of comfort. Washing their quarters was one thing. He thought another might be a drink of rum after their last feed later that afternoon to settle them below for the rest of the day. The captain would have to give his consent to this since rum supplies had to be maintained for the entire journey and became more of an imperative as the length of time at sea grated on everyone's nerves. He'd have to check the rum supplies to see how much, if any, could be spared. The second mate asked Kelsal if he could have a word. Kelsal smiled and said there was something they could do together while they talked.

'What?' the second mate wanted to know.

'Check the rum supplies with me.'

The second mate smiled. 'Certainly, Mr Kelsal.'

Simon stood a few feet from the two men. He heard the word 'rum' and laughed, but next to the word 'supplies' it did not sound as funny to his mind. He stood and watched the two men walk away in the direction of the storeroom. Instead of a room full of supplies he saw a giant version of Mintah curled up in the room with her face filling the door frame. He gasped and bolted below.

The slaves were more defiant than ever. Every instruction had to be backed up with a lash or prod with a club. Kelsal had noticed this mounting resistance in the slaves since the disposals had got underway. The crew too seemed to have abandoned what meagre sense of decorum they had possessed. Kelsal and the second mate walked round the quarterdeck and caught one sailor forcing himself on a pregnant slave in broad daylight in the rain. And the man seemed annoyed with them for disturbing him. Had the captain come upon this scene that sailor would have been clapped in irons, but Kelsal and the second mate knew they could not spare a single hand at present. Both agreed that the slaves needed to see a vigilant crew up to its full complement. Any sign of weakness on the part of the crew would be an opportunity for the slaves to erupt in rebellion. Kelsal promised the sailor a flogging or leg irons later that day. The second mate added a kick to the man's rump, cursed him for his lack of discretion and had the woman return below.

'Now, where were we, Mr Kelsal?' The second mate rocked happily on his bow-legs. 'Oh, yes, the rum supplies . . .'

Vinegar permeated the air below decks. Noses were stung by it. The fumes drifted from the slave hold to the storeroom, where Mintah was practising a series of imaginary tasks to keep her body limber. She seemed to be threshing wheat when she swung her arms above her head and brought them down in a slashing motion in front of her body to within inches of the floor, or else beating clothes with a paddle on the banks of a river. These movements were shortened from an area above her head to chest level, perhaps a pestle pounding a vegetable in a mortar. She refused to dance. When a drum rhythm presented itself she squashed it from her thoughts. Drum and dance would have to wait for a more propitious place.

The sound of key in the door made her run behind the bags of rice and crouch out of sight. Simon called her as if he were being pursued.

'Mintah! You have to get out now! First Mate Kelsal and the second mate are on their way to check the rum.'

Mintah could see from Simon's wide eyes that her discovery in this room would bring down on his head and shoulders more calamity than he could bear. She picked up something Simon could not see in the poor light and ran from the storeroom, heading straight for the women's section of the slave hold. Simon locked the door and had just turned to retrace his steps to the kitchen when he heard the voices of Kelsal and the second mate and they turned the corner and confronted him.

'What are you up to, lad?'

Kelsal's concentrated stare always made Simon shift his weight from one foot to the other as if trying to evade it.

'Nothing, Mr Kelsal.'

'You should always be doing something, lad. There is always something to do on the *Zong*. Come along with us and make yourself useful.'

'Yes, Mr Kelsal.'

The second mate had the cook's key, which he used to enter the storeroom. Simon pointed them to the casks of rum.

'A sailor can always find rum, lad.' The second mate smiled. At the first cask, he and Kelsal waved their empty goblets at Simon and filled them. Then they touched goblets and sipped noisily.

'Rum helps a man count, remember that, lad.'

'Yes, Second Mate.'

'Well, don't just stand there, go ahead and count, lad.'

'I can only count to ten, Second Mate.'

'Good. When you reach ten, tell us, and then count another lot of ten.'

'Yes, Second Mate.'

Simon spread his fingers and began. The first and second mates toasted each other's health. The second mate looked up at Kelsal. 'Someone will have to tell the captain that this has got to stop.'

Kelsal pretended that he did not understand. 'What? Sailors needing a little rum?'

The second mate did not show any outward sign of annoyance, nor did he burst out with his usual guffaw. Kelsal had expected to hear this but he wasn't going to make any promises he couldn't fulfil. He leaned forward to catch the eye of his second mate, 'Look, I know.'

'You are first mate, it's up to you to tell him. The men expect you to.'

'I know.'

Kelsal looked at the floor. His shoulders stooped so low that the second mate took pity on him.

'Don't mind me. I'm just saying what the men are telling me.'

'They are right. You are right. I can't promise anything. I'll try.'

They stood still, drinking up in silence, and looked about the room, careful to avoid each other's eyes.

Mintah heard some movement in the gangway ahead so she crept into the men's section of the slave hold with the index finger of her right hand over her lips. There were shrieks and open mouths and sudden intakes of breath, and several of the sick men, who were not chained, forgot their ailments and bolted across the floor away from her. She explained, in the three coastal languages she knew, how she had grabbed a rope and climbed aboard and had been hiding all this time. In her other hand she showed them a few long nails and a file. The men smiled and nodded. They crept forward and all wanted to talk to her at once. She begged them not to attract the attention of the crew and to tell the men nearer the partition separating them from the women not to reveal anything of her presence. She explained that the sea was no place for her people, and before another living soul could be thrown into it they would do something to prevent it. The men agreed but some said she would lead them to their deaths and a second death for her. That she was blessed by the gods but not invincible. That she should take her madness elsewhere. Even if they gained control of the ship they had no idea which direction to steer it in or how to steer it to get them back to Africa. Give her back the nails and file, she insisted, and she would go and seek the help of the women. If they were content with lying in their misery they did not deserve to see Africa again. But the man with the file had already started to cut through his chain linking him to his partner. And the others with the nails were trying to break open the locks on their anklets. Mintah stopped them and explained that they were not to free themselves right away. They should conceal the file and nails until they got her signal.

Mintah moved deeper into the hold wishing everyone well and the men touched her for some of her magic to rub off on them and to check that she wasn't an apparition. She asked them not to do anything until they had freed as many men as possible. They should post a lookout and speak to the women they could trust, since some women were free to move about the ship and perform various chores, placing them in an ideal position to steal a weapon. She would have to show herself to a few of the women otherwise rumours of her survival would be dismissed. Her access to the women's section was blocked by a partition, extended and reinforced recently by the crew. Whereas, previously, an adult could squeeze through the gaps at the sides, now only a hand could get around it. She looked again and saw that a child's body might squeeze through. One of the men called a child by name, and the boy came up to the gap: an arm and leg appeared through it and then a head and the rest of the boy. He stood there looking pleased with his feat but dived back towards the gap with a screech when he saw Mintah. It was the boy who had nearly been thrown over the side. He knew the sea meant death and was certain that with Mintah's death he would not see her again. What stood before him must therefore be a spirit. Mintah held him and explained about the rope and the fins that came after her and her climb up the side of the slimy hull to safety. At last the boy looked at her face and he returned her embrace. Mintah explained that he should go back and send out the girl who was with him on deck yesterday. The boy told Mintah that the girl had been thrown into the sea that morning and they would never see her again. Mintah could not stop the tears gathering in her eyes and overflowing. She bit her lip, swiped the wetness off her face with her index fingers and asked the boy to get another child to squeeze through the gap.

He left and came back but there were now several voices with him. A girl pushed her head into the men's section, saw Mintah and retreated. Mintah called her to come back but the gap remained empty. Then another girl, older than the last, pushed her head through and saw that what the boy had said was true. She stretched out her arm and ran it over Mintah's face and hair and then disappeared. Soon women's hands came into the gap and Mintah placed herself next to it and they felt her head, her face, her body. And she spoke to them.

'I am Mintah. I was thrown into the sea and grabbed a rope and climbed up the ship to safety.'

The talk grew loud. Several women rushed to the partition to feel Mintah and hear her for themselves. Mintah backed away from the partition when a couple of the crew shouted into the women's section for them to quieten down. She withdrew to the door of the men's hold ready to leave. An old man asked her why she wanted them to wait instead of freeing themselves immediately. She replied that there would be a sign from her and they should wait for it. What sign? he wanted to know. Two of the men said they would not wait for a woman to lead them to certain death. If anything was to be done it had to happen right away.

Just then Simon peered into the hold and retreated. Right away Mintah stepped from behind the door and rushed after him.

'Simon.'

'Mintah?' He spun round and sighed with relief. 'They're gone, let's go.'

He trotted to the storeroom, leading Mintah by the

hand. As soon as she was through the door, he locked it and rushed for the kitchen. Mintah slumped down on to the floor and clasped her arms around her knees and thought about the little girl that she had saved to live another day, only to see more things no child should see, only to end up in the sea. And how would that child find her way home? Her last cry poured into the sea. Her small bones adding to a sea of bones.

Kelsal was back on deck with his second mate. The crewman who had earlier been caught with a pregnant woman in a compromising position, had the woman by his side when he addressed Kelsal. She was eating bread that he'd given her.

'First Mate Kelsal, listen to what my friend here has to say.'

Through her actions and the occasional English word the Ashanti woman described how the woman who went by the name Mintah, the one who kept calling 'Kelsal, Kelsal,' and who was thrown over the side yesterday, her spirit was now on board, roaming the ship. She had seen it and felt it and it had a body and the warmth of the living person that Mintah once was. Kelsal could not believe his ears. He declared that she was mad and so was the sailor for listening to her. If she could make this fantastic claim for a piece of bread, the second mate wondered, what would she reveal for some rum? The woman was insistent. She pulled her hair just as Mintah had pulled Kelsal's. She grabbed a rope and mimicked climbing along it. Kelsal looked at her again, then he walked to the side and looked over at the array of dangling ropes.

'Surely you don't believe her?' The second mate threw up his hands. But Kelsal was already calling the captain and the boatswain.

He made her repeat everything. They all shook their

heads in disbelief. Other women were questioned and, although most were silent, a few confirmed, more out of defiance than anything else, that they had indeed touched Mintah's head, face, hand, body; had heard Mintah's voice in the men's section of the hold. The captain told everyone to remain calm and to follow him in a little investigation. He reminded them not to forget the source of this rumour: the Africans were mightily superstitious and this most recent frenzy was probably a figment of their inventive, idle minds.

Captain Cunningham beckoned his officers to accompany him below. He led the way down into the hold with a handkerchief pressed to his mouth and nose. His eyes watered with the acridity. He swallowed to stop himself from retching, then stopped and grabbed Kelsal's arm. The crewmen sidled pass them. Captain Cunningham clenched his teeth, squeezed his eyes shut several times, released his grip on Kelsal and pressed forward. They burst into the men's section holding up lamps and clubs. Two of the men's chains were loose, their shackles open and removed. The first and second mate, the boatswain and two sailors grabbed the men and called for chains and fetters to be brought.

Captain Cunningham pointed his whip at a man on the floor with Kelsal's knee pressed into his back.

'Mintah. Where is she?'

'No Mintah.'

'Bring him out. Secure the other one. Check them all.'

Three crew came into the hold and began an inspection of the men's chains.

'Something is amiss, gentlemen. We shall soon learn what.'

On deck in the drizzle, thumbscrews were applied to

the man and Mintah's name repeated as the screws were tightened.

The screws crushed his nails and punctured the flesh of his thumbs. A red pool gathered on both thumbs and overflowed. The man cried and shouted, 'Mintah gone!'

'Where is she? Where?'

'Mintah gone.'

'All right, that's enough. He's not going to talk.'

The thumbscrews were removed and the man was chained hand to foot and returned to the hold in this crouching position. The crew added more chains to the men, already linked in pairs by their ankles, by chaining them hands to feet. Only the very sick were exempted.

The captain ordered an immediate search of the vessel. 'Feed them below. And no rum.' He paced back and forth, peered over the side and saw the ropes for himself, but still couldn't see how a woman could have fallen into the sea and managed to get hold of one. He reminded himself that she was not sick like the rest of them. Nevertheless he opened his ledger to the entry he had made for one sick woman thrown overboard and crossed it out. He cursed aloud, still doubting the evidence of his ears, 'She was a woman, damn it!'

Below, in the children's section of the hold, the boy who had been saved by Mintah and who had seen her for himself told the other children that they would be saved by her. As he spoke he moved about the cramped space and patted other children on the back who were older than himself. His face shone with conviction. He described how she had killed three of the big fish with the fins before taming a fourth and riding on its back by holding on to its fin, had got the man-eating fish to swim after the ship and catch up with it, and then how she had scaled the hull with her bare hands and feet. Mintah was on the ship and they would be safe. She would break the chains of the men between her teeth and they would all be free. She had told him that they should help each other, try to be happy and eat all their food, even if it tasted like poison.

To the women, talking among themselves, Mintah's reappearance was nothing short of a miracle. The gods were present in her to watch over them. How else could a woman be thrown into the big sea and climb back on to a speeding ship? Hadn't she assumed the invisibility of a god to remain on board all this time undetected? Which goddess was she? How would it all end? When the gods interfered in the affairs of people there was no telling how things would turn out. Lucky for them this god was on their side. Not so lucky for the crew or those who had betrayed her.

Some of the women began to clap and sing an improvised song in which they took turns to praise Mintah's name.

'Mintah is a god who walks among us as a woman.'

'Aieee!' Whistles, ululations and rapid clapping which then slowed for the next encomium.

'A god has come as Mintah to save us from this sea.'

'Aieee!' More whistles and ululating and fast handclaps.

'The goddess Mintah will free this ship and guide it back to Africa.' Aieees! Endless whistles, ceaseless ululations, clapping and clapping as if it were not conjecture but had come true.

Each of them conjured up a picture of home, images they had tried over the weeks to bury inside since all they had felt was misery when they'd dug them up. Now they could cherish them again. All the villages and towns and everyone they had seen in them, all the animals and birds, the rivers and valleys, mountains and forests could be entertained now. Their days and nights on the land had been merely suspended. They were not as good as dead. This water had a beginning and an end. They were destined to step off this ship on to dry land. If Mintah could return from the sea, they could live to feel land underfoot. They shouted these things, less to each other and more as a gesture to empty the hold of despair and fill the sea. The same few lines arose in a song that was taken up by some of the women, who sang it until it spread through the women's hold and stirred even the sick from their stupor. A woman too sick to raise herself on to her elbows simply allowed herself the rarity of a smile and rocked her head from side to side and mouthed the words.

> We are on the sea
> Not in the sea
>
> Over the sea
> Not under the sea
>
> Apart from the sea
> Not a part of the sea
>
> Show us mercy
> Mintah's mercy
>
> And show us land
> Mintah's land

The children would have nothing to do with the celebrations. Their movements quickened and their eyes widened in the dark section of their compartment, at the prospect that grown women had come to this, but none of them sang or clapped their hands, even though many of those women were their mothers and they could

94

pick out their voices among the chorus. All this joy would bring something crashing down on their heads. They had to brace themselves for that. There were no grown-ups between them and what would be visited on them next. All they had to rely on was themselves. They shivered at the thought that whatever would happen would have something to do with the sea. There was Mintah, but where were all the rest? Their bodies had to be prepared to meet the sea. Not with song. With silence. With listening in the dark. To what surrounded them. Raged all around them. To break in on their cramped world and snatch them from it.

Chapter Six

THERE NOW BEGAN a methodical search of the *Zong*. The crew fanned out across the main deck and the quarterdeck and looked into every nook, cranny and interstice. Men clambered down ropes despite the high sea and weak late afternoon light to inspect the sloop and two smaller boats. Tarpaulins spread over cannons and lookout posts were lifted and poked with staves to detect flesh. Below decks the officers' and captain's quarters were turned over. A man looking in a drawer was reprimanded by the second mate for defying reason.

Secret supplies of cheese and tobacco, rum and sugar were discovered in the crew's quarters, resulting in fines and threats to the crew from the captain and officers. At the storeroom the captain and boatswain were through the door when both first and second mates caught up with them and vouched that they had been over it already. The party moved on to the mess and the galley, where the cook opened large vats for them to look into and the crew speculated that the evening meal might include their ghostly interloper.

All eyes were on the captain as they waited for the next order. He was pacing the main deck. He looked as if he was nursing a baby and trying to soothe it the way he had his arms clasped round the ledger, and from his occasional downward glances at it.

'Resume the disposals of the sick pieces and let them know we will not stop with the sick, if this Mintah does not surrender.'

The crew sighed. In the past they had been assigned to duties for which they had little appetite, but this dumping of livestock overboard was hard to stomach. They told each other in hushed tones that if the poor wretched creatures were to die anyway, why not leave them in a corner to die? Why go through all this fussing and fighting with them when the same outcome – their death – would consign their bodies to the sea, and his precious ledger, which he cared about more than anyone, could record the fact of the death and disguise the exact circumstances. Everyone's life would be easier if dead stock were thrown over the side instead of live stock. They agreed someone should have a quiet word in the ear of the first or second mate, but not the boatswain.

Two groups of three were named by the second mate, one under his leadership, the other to be guided by First Mate Kelsal. The captain waited beneath his makeshift shelter with his ledger. Rain continued to pound the deck. The southeast trades picked up. The crewman who had learned of Mintah's presence on the ship from the superstitious pregnant woman asked Mr Kelsal if he had a moment. Kelsal was about to descend into the hold. He spun round and leaned towards the sailor, who was a small man and so seemed dwarfed by Kelsal's stooped shoulders towering over him.

'Not now, sailor. We have a job to do.'

The man was silent for a moment, long enough for Kelsal to turn away, then, encouraged by the preferred sight of Kelsal's back, he said, 'It concerns this so-called job, Mr Kelsal.'

Kelsal stopped and focused his gaze on the sailor who, like the cook's assistant, began to shift from one foot to the other as if to dodge the full impact of Kelsal's stare. The first mate wondered why his face made men uneasy. As things stood it was an asset.

'The men feel that it is bad to throw the helpless sick overboard. Troublemakers and mutineers among the stock, like that female Mintah, are another matter. But this dumping is cruel and endless and more than the men can bear. Would you, Mr Kelsal, on the men's behalf tell the captain our minds?'

Captain Cunningham wondered what the conference was about. Every order issued by him in the last day or so seemed to necessitate lengthy debate. He might as well have stayed at home and issued written decrees and left it to the whim of the sailors to decide which to obey and which to disregard. His jaw worked convulsively. His knuckles whitened around his grip on the ledger.

'What's the delay over there, Mr Kelsal?'

Kelsal looked over at the captain, then back at the sailor.

'I will not, sailor.'

The man looked shocked and displeased. He spat on the deck and ground in the result then joined his designated group and conveyed to them the news of Kelsal's refusal to represent them to the captain.

'Is there a problem, First Mate Kelsal?'

'No, Captain.'

The allotted crew filed into the men's section of the hold, announced that Mintah was the cause of their misery, and picked out two sick men, who kicked and punched and bit the crew and had to be gagged and bound hand and foot, before being taken above and summarily dumped over the side.

Fins in the ship's wake dipped out of sight. Blood darkened the trail of the ship and spread wider into the sea. Captain Cunningham added two strokes to his ledger and looked up from it to see another two men in chains struggling with the crew. Another two men hoisted off the deck and over the side. And two more. And two women who screamed and begged and then kicked and started to bite and spit. Then another two who had to be thrown on the deck and bound and gagged then lifted and rushed to the side and flung over. And two children who shrieked and whose eyes were ready to pop from their sockets at what was happening to them. They were not ready for the sea.

'Mintah!' they cried before vanishing over the side. Their bodies struck the surface of the sea soundlessly and it opened instantly and with hardly a splash they were admitted into it and the opening closed leaving no trace of their ever having been there. Another child managed to wriggle from the clutches of the crew and run from them around the top deck until she was cornered, and as they closed in on her she sat down and buried her eyes in her hands, and screamed, kicking her legs and keeping her hands on her face. She was scooped up by one of the crew, who lifted her high at arm's length to avoid her kicks, and flung her into the sea. Her hands covered her face. But her child's body was cloaked with eyes.

'Enough, Mr Kelsal! Enough!'

The voice surprised Kelsal. It was his second mate blocking his exit up the hatch.

'You stop this madness now!' He gripped Kelsal's arm. Kelsal looked down at the hand in disbelief and kept gazing at it until the second mate slackened his hold and let his arm drop to his side.

Kelsal pushed past him, climbed up on deck, turning his face away from the rain and wind and hunching his shoulders, and walked over to the captain. He did not invite Kelsal under the tarpaulin with a little half-step to one side and a flick of his head to indicate there was room beside him. He stood his ground, raised his eyebrows, looked down at his ledger then up into Kelsal's face. Kelsal could see the captain's jaws working busily, assembling some reprimand. He knew he had to be quick.

'Captain, the men are tired of this undertaking.'

He waited and fixed his gaze on the ledger, squinting to protect his eyes against the wind and rain. The captain looked up at the sky that was nearly as low as the makeshift cover over his head, a sky that had changed little in thirty-six hours and so was unlikely to furnish him with any new revelations. He was searching it for a loan of some of the patience it had demonstrated in its gradual and unrelenting soaking of everything under it. He took so long looking up that Kelsal's gaze travelled after his and, seeing nothing but thick, low-lying cloud, retraced its steps to his tight face.

'All right, Kelsal, let them stop. Forty-two is accept-able for today. We will resume tomorrow.' Captain Cunningham pressed his ledger to his chest in conso-lation, as if some higher authority, represented by the ledger and served by him, had still to be satisfied. Kelsal frowned and did not avert his eyes from the captain's hard stare.

'No, Captain. If I read the mood of the crew correctly there will be no resumption of this distasteful chore tomorrow.'

The captain gritted his teeth and again looked sky-wards. 'Is this ship threatened with mutiny, Kelsal, on account of our handling of stock?'

'Captain, the crew cannot see the point of dumping sick slaves over the side if they might recover or if they are going to die anyway; they do not see the sense in dumping them alive, when in a few days they would be dead and easier to dispose of.'

'And what is your view of this, Kelsal?'

'I feel the same way, Captain.'

The second mate and the boatswain were standing a few feet away trying hard to appear oblivious to what they were overhearing by staring at the heavens and parts of their clothing. The former seemed satisfied, the latter annoyed.

Captain Cunningham called to them to come nearer. They trotted quickly to his side.

'Second Mate, what do you say?'

'I agree with Mr Kelsal, Captain.'

'Boatswain?'

'Captain Cunningham, I am not in agreement with the first and second mate. This is a necessary and profitable decision on your part. I back it completely.'

The captain looked around the deck at the scattered crew and shouted at the weather, 'Would you men be satisfied if the boatswain and I reaped the profits gained from concluding this task ourselves?'

Kelsal could see that the crew were reluctant to speak out. He inhaled deeply, on the crew's behalf it seemed since no one moved. But he began to speak louder than he intended.

'I think, Captain, that all of us, with the exception of the boatswain, will have nothing further to do with this treatment of the sick.'

This drew approving nods from the crew. Captain Cunningham addressed his remarks to them.

'So you are all willing to disobey your captain and sacrifice the profits of this entire voyage because of a distaste for work?'

Kelsal looked at the second mate for help. He took the cue.

'Captain, we feel enough of this disposal has taken place to merit a decent profit.'

'And what if we arrive in Jamaica and parcels of the stock are still sick and they fetch poor prices? Will we have disposed of enough pieces to make up the losses with a claim from the underwriters? Think about this overnight, gentlemen. I have grounds for charging you with mutiny. I am prepared to reduce the number of pieces we need to dispose of in order to accommodate your distaste for this work, but we are not finished. Give me a little of your time tomorrow and this work will be done and we will have money to show for these months away from our families and friends. Refuse me and I am forced to file a suit against the first and second mate for insubordination and the rest of you for behaviour liable to incite a mutiny. I know the companies at Liverpool: you will not sail on another ship if I put your names about in this unfavourable light. Dismissed.'

Captain Cunningham slapped his ledger, plunged it under his cape and left the deck. The crew moved off in small groups, leaving Kelsal and the second mate with the boatswain. The latter dashed towards the captain's quarters.

Simon found Mintah sitting on the floor of the storeroom crying. He sat beside her and told her he had earned enough money to buy her in Jamaica and set her free. He told her Liverpool was a nice place and she could come there with him. People from Africa lived there. And with her good head she could turn her mind to anything. Mintah hugged Simon. She thanked him for hiding her and bringing her meals and even a bucket for her to use which he had taken away for her without complaint. He had brought her soap and a rag to wash herself with and a clean piece of cloth to wrap around her body. His kindness reminded her of the missionaries she had lived with on the coast, and it proved that not all of his people were bad. Simon interrupted her. He said he did not want to hear another word. If she wished it, he would protect her because he loved her. But he thought she needed more time to grow to love him, and time would convince her. Mintah replied that her heart felt love for him too but she could not entertain that aspect of love while there was so much cruelty and suffering around her.

'Simon, when you get back to Liverpool several women will see your goodness and love you for it.'

'Several women?'

'Yes.'

'How do you know?'

'Because if I lived in your Liverpool, a free woman, I would be one of them.'

'But not here?'

'Not here.'

She hugged Simon, whose head spun with elation at having his good fortune told by a reliable source, and depression at having his scheme to save Mintah declined. He left her with the last meal of the day, a mixture of rice and yams topped with a sauce of ground peppers, salt and palm oil. She did not hear him lock the door and chose not to remind him. The second his footsteps died away she left the storeroom, knowing she had to act quickly while the crew were all busy racing against the gathering dusk to

103

finish their duties before it became too dark. She ate from her bowl as she swayed along the gangway, ducking out of sight when a couple of women passed her with buckets of food, and when the way seemed clear stepping into the men's section.

The stench of the enclosed quarters put Mintah off the rest of her meal. She put down her bowl, straightened up as high as she could without hitting her head on the low ceiling and blinked in the confined darkness. Voices shouted above the noise of chains. Men pushed each other out of the way and grabbed at the buckets of food. The food was forgotten when the men saw Mintah – a lull that gave the weaker men an opportunity to help themselves. Mintah asked everyone if they believed that anything would be gained by her surrender to the crew. Several of the men said they thought the murders of the sick would come to an end if the captain saw her for himself. Others argued that the crew would do with her as they pleased then carry on as they pleased with the sick, that nothing was to be gained by her subjecting herself to torments at their hands. One of the older men wondered if she could negotiate with the captain to cease the killings in return for their cooperation for the remainder of the voyage.

'These people only negotiate with Africans if we have slaves to sell them.'

'Things are worse because of Mintah – she should surrender.'

'No! Remain in hiding. At least one of us will escape torture.'

Mintah held up a pike. It was strong enough to break open the locks of the fetters around the men's hands and feet with one twist.

'Tell me to take this weapon away and I will go with it and you will never hear from me again.'

Several men shouted that she should get out, instead of bringing down more trouble on their heads. Others buried their heads in despair. But most of them held out their hands for the pike. Mintah kneeled beside the nearest hand. It belonged to a young man whom she had noticed on her last visit. He was strong and commanded the attention of the men around him when he spoke. She positioned the pike in the lock on his ankle, and when he nodded she yanked it as he pushed on it and the lock broke. The young man rubbed his ankle, stretched out his leg and smiled at Mintah. She handed the pike to him and asked him to free a group of men with his strength and courage.

Saying she would return in a moment, Mintah dashed into the women's section. The strongest of the women were supervising the fair distribution of the food between the healthy and the sick. The women fell silent. A couple of them advanced and ordered Mintah to give herself up and bring their misery to an end. Mintah stood her ground and told them their misery was caused by the cruelty of the crew and not by her presence on the ship. A bunch of women jumped to Mintah's defence and said she was blessed by the gods and would bring them luck whatever she did. They asked her what she wanted them to do, for they would willingly die for a god.

'Too many of us have died already. Let us put a stop to the killing of the sick,' she told them.

When they heard the signal every woman who was not sick should block the path of the crew. They should do everything to stop the crew from arming themselves. Those women who were free to walk around the deck should position themselves near the cannon and the look-out posted above the quarterdeck, and at the first sign of a fight they were to stop the lookout from firing his gun and the crew from firing the cannon. Any woman not in agreement with her should remain in the hold and comfort the children.

Mintah returned to the men. By now four of them were free and were at work on the chains of others. Many men refused to have their chains broken. They said that when this latest madness was put down by the crew all those who were not in chains would bring awful punishments on themselves. As it was, the very attempt would worsen conditions for everyone.

Mintah said there was no time for arguments. Those who were not sick should imagine what it was like waiting to be picked up and flung overboard. She knew what it was like and therefore did not want another sick person to experience it. The men who were too sick to participate nodded their consent. This silenced the dissenters.

'Let's go!'

The four young men bunched behind Mintah. One had a pike ready. Nails were gripped by the three others. She had brought more nails and a second pike from the storeroom after the crew's search of the hold had resulted in the confiscation of her earlier supply of these weapons. The man with the pike walked in front of Mintah and held out the pike to show that he was armed and therefore should lead. Mintah nodded. They ran to the hatch, gave each other one last look and climbed to the main deck.

They met the wind and the rain. The last of the twilight shone on them. They grabbed a crewman who was walking past and was too surprised even to scream. The pike was brought down on his head several times while the others tore his skin with their nails. His blood spread across the deck and ran along the grooves between the planks in the rain. His cutlass and club were pulled from his body and the men ran towards another sailor, who turned on his heel and bolted. A blow from the cutlass caught him on the back of the head and he sprawled on the deck and rolled until he came to rest against the side. He held his cutlass but was too slow to draw it. The men clubbed him and chopped him around his head and shoulders. His hands came up and his left arm was chopped clean through by the cutlass swung by one of the men. He looked at his arm. Mintah signalled them to stop. The sailor swayed on his knees. Mintah grabbed him and the men helped her lift him. They hoisted him high into the air, screamed in triumph and threw him over the side. A pistol fired and one of the young men staggered as he was hit with partridge shot. Mintah turned. She saw five of the crew advancing armed with pistols. The captain pushed to the front and spoke.

'Drop your weapons or you will all die right where you stand!'

Mintah looked to her left and saw the boatswain and the second mate with pistols. The cannon on the quarterdeck was being aimed at them and a lighted fuse was ready. Kelsal scrambled forward armed with a pistol and a club. Mintah held up her arms and told the men to lower their weapons. The crew pulled the cutlasses, club, pike and nails from the hands of the men and Mintah. The captain raised his pistol to chest level and waved it in the air.

'Tie them! They are not to be harmed!'

Protests arose from the crew. The second mate shouted, 'But two of our men are dead, Captain!'

Captain Cunningham pointed his pistol at the second mate.

'I said tie them! They are healthy. They will fetch more in Jamaica than any insurance can pay. If another man questions my orders I swear I will shoot him!'

The crew shook their heads, spat, and glared at the

captain, looking to Kelsal for some word, only to get his nod of assent.

The four men and Mintah were bound hand and foot. They were pushed into a sitting position on the deck, arranged back to back in a rough circle and a rope was tied around them. A crew member was assigned to guard them while the others went to lock the women below and to check on the men. They removed all the food buckets and beat any male slave not in chains. All hatches were secured and the ship stopped by spilling the wind from the sails.

Next, they wrapped the dead crewman in his hammock and stitched it up, including a piece of pig iron at his feet for ballast. Everyone bowed his head as the Captain read from his prayer book, 'Into thy hands, O merciful Saviour, we commend thy servant, William Pelling . . .' Two of the crew who were friendly with the dead man cried, inviting pats from those around them. '. . . A sinner of thine own redeeming.' Mintah and the four men bound together watched and listened. '. . . Suffer us not, at our last hour, through any pains of death, to fall from thee.'

The sailors uttered a collective, 'Amen.'

Captain Cunningham closed his prayer book and opened his Bible. 'Out of the deep have I called to Thee O Lord . . .' Mintah's head filled with the sick who had been thrown overboard. She sobbed. Could not look. '. . . Lord hear my voice . . .' The boatswain blew his whistle. It gargled, choked with rain. He flicked his hand twice and plugged the whistle back into his mouth. This time its shrill pierced the air. The plank holding the carapaced body was angled out over the side and tilted and William Pelling slid off it and the sea swallowed.

The captain spoke to his men about the importance of a successful conclusion to the voyage, then he walked over to Mintah, roped together with her four accomplices.

'Tell me how you got back on board and how you evaded capture despite a complete search of the *Zong*.'

Mintah stared up at the captain's face, dripping rain and burned red by the wind.

'Promise me we will not be harmed and that you will not throw another living soul overboard and I will tell you what you want to know.'

'I can promise you all your lives. You are all healthy, and you will fetch good prices at the market, but I cannot guarantee the lives of those sick and dying.'

'Then kill me, Captain, because I do not want to live if they must die at your hands.'

The captain raised his arm to strike Mintah. She pushed her head towards him and glared. He froze with his arm upraised. Then he straightened, jerked his arms in front of him, shook his head and stormed to his quarters, beckoning Kelsal, the second mate and the boatswain to follow him. The three stood in a semi-circle in the cramped space in silence, glad to be out of the rain. Captain Cunningham surprised them all by reaching for his brandy. With swift dips of the decanter he filled four goblets, his hands trembling, and handed one to each of the men in turn. He raised the fourth to them. The others reciprocated the gesture and drained their cups. Captain Cunningham filled them again.

'We cannot throw all our slaves away, gentlemen, but we can as a form of punishment continue with the disposal of the remainder of the sick. We can punish a few of them as an example to the others and secure peace for the rest of this voyage. Do not reply now. Take the evening to consider it. In the morning we can decide. But those five are among our healthiest stock. They must not be harmed. Agreed?'

'Yes, Captain!' The boatswain was loudest of the three. Captain Cunningham searched the faces of the first and second mates and both nodded their assent and left. Kelsal lingered by the door, afraid it seemed to return to the wet wind.

'What is it, First Mate?'

Kelsal remained facing the door but peered round at the captain. 'Captain, if we resume the dumpings we may or may not be punishing the slaves but we will certainly punish the crew.'

The captain threw his goblet across the room and slammed his fist on the table. 'You are bent on seeing this mission fail, Kelsal, that is plain for all to see. But this order of mine will be carried out with or without your cooperation.'

Kelsal looked out at the rain and shrugged.

'Get out, Kelsal.'

Canvas was thrown over the heads of Mintah and the four men. When it occurred to him and when he was sure he was unobserved, the man assigned to watch them would take a surreptitious swing with his club at the covered bodies. Later that evening, after a long meeting with the captain, when both men could be heard shouting, Kelsal walked out into the dark and told the watch that if he saw any blood on the slaves in the morning the watch would have to account for it and face the consequences.

Chapter Seven

FINGERS OF RAIN thrummed on the canvas and a powerful body braced against it on all sides and hummed and whistled as if to gain admission or to keep Mintah and the four men captive with a mixture of force and charm. Where the canvas did not touch the deck a stream finding its way around an obstacle managed to run straight through followed by the humming. Both felt cold on skin. Both induced shivers. The five bodies viewed the two elements as their enemies. Something to defend against. So they huddled even closer than their chains dictated. A song of their own surfaced on one pair of lips and was picked up by the others and became an anthem against the tapping and singing around them. To compensate for the ship's tilt to leeward they had their necks and heads angled like dandelions tracking the sun. And they swayed with the ship which swayed to the rhythm of the sea. Permeating all these was night, gathered into a thick drape and thrown over the world. Night brought the horizon, round as a coin and far off by day, close to the ship's prow. The dark sea skulked through this solid pitch blackness, powered and extended by it. The *Zong* felt its way along like someone blindfolded with outstretched hands in an unfamiliar furnished room. Except that the sea kept moving its furniture around. Kept introducing inclines, steps and sudden drops in its floor so that the *Zong* crashed into things with every move and only made progress because the shapes it hit eventually and reluctantly yielded to it.

The sea was endless. Because it kept the horizon at a distance or else so close that both seemed the same, Mintah believed they were adrift on it rather than heading towards land. The rest of her days would be passed here. She would never be still again. She would not know what it was to measure her destination against a landscape again. Those who died must have perished with the belief that the land was the past and the sea was the present; that there was no future. The sea was the beginning and end of everything. In the dark it made each lurch of the *Zong* seem like the last. But there was always another so close to the one just experienced that it erased the former immediately, making it seem that only one movement ever occurred, that rather than being a succession of jolts there was just the one unending action. Up to now she had thought something could be done to halt this perpetual movement on the spot and somehow throw it into reverse and recapture what she and everyone held captive on the *Zong* had had before. A place to leave and return to in light or shadow. A geography with fixed points, however remote.

Instead, she was lost. At sea. Lost to her name. Her body. She felt cold or else numb. Soon she would feel nothing at all. Truly lost. What remained? Her companions. She leaned harder against them. Allowed her head to fall more heavily on the other heads. Savoured their warmth. Recognised in the few lines about home that they repeated together something this sea could never own even though they were in its clutches and at its mercy and might end up in it.

She began to feel warm or ceased to feel the cold. Either way, she was aware that she no longer shivered. She saw herself in front of a fire in a compound filled to capacity. The fingers on the canvas and the whistle in the wind and the lashing of the sea plaited their sibilance and became speech. An elder was explaining how things would be between the kingdom and the men from the sea. How this slavery that had divided and destroyed many people would be ended by this new plan. The answer lay in working the land around them. Planting, right there, the sugar cane, cotton, tobacco, tea and coffee that these foreigners valued enough to kill each other for. Harvesting and loading those crops into the foreigners' ships, instead of filling the ships with men, women and children and sending them to faraway lands to work for the same ends.

From this, and from seeing the offspring of unions between white men and black women, and the many tribes who trafficked in captive souls for riches, grew her conviction that if the whites had come and settled in Africa and hired Africans to work African soil and grow the very crops they deemed so valuable that they were willing to cast their humanity aside in order to procure them in abundance and gain riches fast, the whole encounter between black and white would have been pleasant and beneficial for all concerned.

The flame that filled her head dwindled to a point of light surrounded by dark, then to nothing but the dark enveloped by coldness. Fingers on the canvas formed into a fist, foot, or the end of a club and thumped her. She shrank from the blow, fought to catch her breath, tried to continue with the song and failed. Fingers returned their pitter-patter on her head and body. She heard the muffled blow on another part of the canvas and felt someone's body bracing against hers, contracting from the blow, making hers contract too. The singing stopped in that person as well. Mintah resumed the song. His lack of breath compelled her to breathe.

> We are on water far from home
> We have been on water forever
> It seems we are all alone,
> We are not and water isn't home,
> Can never be home; not now or ever.

Her eyes were closed. She heard herself and the others above the roaring of the wind and the rain. The way they moved with the ship matched their song. Without sight of a fire Mintah still felt warmth. Heat generated by the feel of the others, and by the song, made her indifferent to the wind and water and to the thumps that replaced them at intervals. She no longer cringed in expectation of a blow as a dog might in proximity to a cruel master. Unable to feel anything but warmth, her body seemed disconnected from the deck and afloat. Not just hers but the whole group she was chained to appeared to rise above the deck. The fingers changed from hitting her to prising her off the deck. Wind no longer pushed and braced against her but lifted her and her companions. They were airborne. Bodiless. She was aware of their flight and of weighing only as much as that awareness might weigh, which was less than a feather in the wind. Breathing was easy. The constriction from the chains eased too. She felt she could part from her companions and stand and stretch if she wished. Dancing was a possibility in this elevating rain and wind. But she did not want to dance. The sensation of being afloat was still too much of a novelty to swap for some new activity, so she relished it, revelled in it. Allowed her head to fall back even more against the heads of her companions and her back to brace against theirs and sang.

Even on land she had not felt this sense of bodilessness. The sea did not offer itself to her as an alternative. She was above it. Floating, the way a bird with outspread wings can appear nailed to one spot in the sky. When the numbness vanished, when her flight ended, she wanted to alight, not on the deck, nor in the sea, not even in the rain. First she wanted to feel soil, mud, stone, rock, clay, sand, loam, pebbles, boulders, grass. Then wood. There must be water. But in a stream or river. Water she could see her face in and a face she could drink. There would be a path she could take and footsteps she would be able to retrace, a path she might choose to look back along and see what progress she had made, or ahead to confirm her destination. One with old roots and stones jutting above the ground to stub the toes against and holes to jolt the first careless foot stepping into them.

If she could lie in mud she would roll in it and don it like a garment, thread it through her hair, lace it between her fingers and toes, wear its mask. She would roll a pebble of it and store it under her tongue until she spoke the language of mud, of soil, of sand. Then she would dry in the sun and become white as stone, solid as the ground she walked on, a rock that had sprung limbs and a head. Wherever she went, earth would be with her because she would have become inseparable from it. Land would figure in her dreams like a lover or friend or parent. An enemy would have to contend with both her and it. And if she were to lie still among rocks, in mud, on sand, she would be indistinguishable from earth, invisible as anything but rock or stone, mud or sand, and therefore beyond the clutches of an enemy.

Once she had made a hole in the ground by pushing a stick down as far as her strength allowed and taking care not to break it. She was copying the grown-ups who plunged sticks into the ground with all their might, except their sticks were bigger and seemed to go deeper into the ground. Like her stick theirs came to a standstill too. And even after they hammered them, their sticks stopped sinking and were in danger of breaking if hit any more. The fence that the adults built was strong despite their sticks coming to a stop in the ground. But Mintah wondered what lay beyond those hammer blows, what secrets the earth kept in its darkest depths. The ground, and what lay beneath it, deep in it, fascinated her more than the moon and the stars. The life that the earth gave to seeds, the wood that it made and held up to the sky, were clues about the world hidden deep in it.

Everything she dreamed, all the shapes without a basis in the waking world that surrounded her, belonged deep in the soil. Wood worked by her hands had tried to find these shapes. Sleep was a descent into the ground. She moved underground like a root feeling its way along, but with more speed, and secreted herself among those shapes, curling around them and caressing them. But waking she often lost all that she had held in her dreams. All that remained was a sensation, a flavour or smell or some pleasure she could not define.

She felt her body on the deck and the familiar rocking motion of the ship and knew she had lost whatever the ground had offered her as she slept and dreamed. Her body was heavy again. The way the ship leaned there was nothing to stop them from being tipped into the sea except the wood they sat on and the way they braced their backs against each other. The sea leapt up the sides of the ship to claim them. Losing patience with them for taking so long to deliver themselves up to it. Surrender to its depths. Find its secrets. Become loose-limbed like water. As boneless. Learn that home is always some other shore. Sink from sunlight and moonlight. Maybe see the stars distended on water, from below water. Or the constellation spread out on a moonlit sea. Remember land like a previous life. Imagine a return until a taste of soil springs up on the tongue and its perfume haunts the nose.

Mintah opened her eyes and looked at a space by her feet where the canvas fell short of the deck. She saw how the dark thinned and was succeeded by grey. Water running by the gap became muscled and sinewy in this first light. Rain dimpled the water. Wind dented it. She lifted the canvas another inch with her bound hands and saw more of the deck, how the water made the wood look wobbly and pliable. Higher still and she saw the feet of the crewman assigned to watch her sticking out of tarpaulin erected into a rough tented structure. A little higher and there was his sleeping face, his folded arms rising and falling on his chest. He was sitting on a stool and his back leaned against the quarterdeck. A club and cutlass lay beside him. She had not seen any of the crew asleep before. His face looked plain, his skin somewhat worn by the salt and the sun. What kept her watching his face was its expressionlessness. She expected to see worries and troubles there brought to the surface of the skin by unguarded sleep. Instead she was faced with peace, plain and simple. How could peace settle on that face? She was appalled at the possibility. She wanted to hit that face and chase peace away. If she knew a way to plant the events of the last two days into that head as it slept so that all that pervaded it were those hours and its events she would do it without hesitation. That face would then be forced to relive every moment of what had transpired before it in its waking hours. Not escape all it had done right in the middle of what it intended to continue. Without waking him she would have him sleep below decks in chains with no room to turn. While preserving his sleep she would thrust his head under sea water and hold it there till his lungs burned with the sea. Then she would have him open his eyes under water while he slept and believe the sea was the last thing he would see. Or show him his land and convince him he would never see it again. That was the sleep she wished for this face, not the one she saw displayed before her, softening its features into a child's, except for the ravages of sun and salt on the skin.

Everything that he did in each passing moment propelled him towards home. Knowing that he would get there at some point, that no matter how long he stayed away or how far he sailed from it he would return one day, must make peace judge his face a proper place to settle on during rest. Not so for those who had left home with no obvious prospect of return. Whose land with each passing moment was thrown farther and farther behind them, swallowed by a horizon leaving no trace or any clues to how it might be recovered. Peace read all this on such a face and veered away from it.

Mintah let the canvas fall over that face and body. Her gaze settled on the water running off the deck, on the burgeoning light playing in that water. If the fingers on the canvas would only hoist her and her companions up, away from salt water, towards a breeze off a mountain or out of a valley or one driven over a plain so that it arrived at a village all sandy and grainy and only found a population willing to shield their faces from it. They would find a way to climb the ladder offered by the rain up to the solid ground of the clouds and walk those clouds, peering through them from time to time until the sea ended and they saw land below. Then they would wait for the clouds to open up, throw down their ladders again. And they would descend those ladders into various compounds, yards, fields, and paths beside someone who recognised them and who would be startled by the surprising route of their return even as they were thankful.

But rainwater returned to the sea, gathered the morning light about itself for its journey to salt water. The sea was its natural ally. Just as wood was Mintah's. She had to rely on wood to get her off the sea no matter where she ended up. Breeze against the canvas and wood pushed them somewhere that meant the end of sea. And the end of the sea was the beginning of home. She was Mintah – mud, sand, dirt, rock, stone. She knew how to bring out the hidden shapes in wood by obeying the wood's grain; the flow of its grain. Shapes from her sleep were buried in wood for her to find; shapes hidden underground, that were the secrets of the earth, surfaced inside wood and were there for her to uncover. Land would be there for her to do these things. Sea threatened to keep her to itself. With each day that she sailed farther from what she knew and loved, some other thing that was strange, that was not the sea, but the sea's end, presented itself. Wood had to be there. Soil she could grow to know. An earth willing to yield something of itself to her.

Mintah felt her companions stir, small movements, within the confines of their chains; their bodies waking to the reality of restriction after a brief respite. Awareness returned to find numbness and aches only, searched every pore of the body for some neutral feeling and could come upon nowhere comfortable to settle and take in its surroundings, therefore was forced to flit from one part of the body to another, alighting and taking flight again. Except for the bracing of backs and the inclined heads where there was warmth and rest. All those aches and that numbness were forgotten. The mind could rest there in those backs braced against each other, in those heads touching. In one move, light flowered around them into water, wood and the sound of the wind and the sea. Light smelled of the sea. Salted light. It coated the tongue and clogged the pores of the skin. Salt scratched at the corners of the eyes; light narrowed them to slits.

The canvas was pulled off them and the tapping fingers landed on their bodies and they shrank from the drumming, unmediated by canvas, as much as from the salt-lash of the light. Mintah looked up at the face that was asleep not so long ago. She barely recognised its features. Awake it had hardened into a series of edges and points that were shuffled around it as it barked at them. There wasn't the least trace of the peace she'd seen there while it slept. Yet peace had holidayed there. And now that face was at war again. Not with the sea, nor the wind and the rain, but with her and her companions. She searched it for the promise of land that kept it going in its hardness and enabled it to savour peace, and could find nothing there that suited her. Its land would not be hers. Wherever it would eventually come to rest she would not. In part, it held her responsible for its discomfort so far from home. Asleep, it may very well have been at home, which is why peace may have mistaken it for a kind place to decorate.

The face multiplied. With their hard edges and points shuffling about them as they grimaced and shouted, they resembled a rough sea, Mintah thought. Slaves who served the sea, forced to traverse it and nourish it with the captured bodies of her people, and to be themselves fed to it when they succumbed to disease or accident or murder. These faces had been away from land for such long periods the sea had become their home. They mimicked its motions like a child studying the movements of a parent. They devoted their waking hours to satisfying the sea, placating it in case it intended to claim them for its next meal. They put Mintah and the other slaves between themselves and the insatiable sea. Their faces hardened under the sun and the salt, against the memory of land. Land was where they could never find peace again. Would not recognise its still contours for anything but damnation. A frozen sea. A dead sea. A sea where they would have to make their own way instead of being conveyed, pitched along, twisted this way and that, with no notion where they'd end up if not on the seabed, with their faces pressed in coral or sand and seaweed braided in their hair and a contentment softening those edges and points as if they'd tricked peace into settling for them once and for all, when in fact they were the ones who'd settled for the sea as home with no thought for peace nor the idea of land, having banished both from their minds except when they fell asleep and could control neither.

Mintah and her companions were unshackled and pulled to their feet. Buckets of rain, scooped from over-flowing water barrels, were thrown at them. They were given soap to scrub themselves. Clubs steered them in one direction and back again for exercise. A whip flicked at their heels and made them hop and skip. Bowls were pushed into their faces and the porridge steamed in the rainwater and they were nudged in the sides to eat. Eat or be eaten by the whip, the club, the chain and shackle. Eat or be eaten by the sea.

Chapter Eight

'SHACKLE THEM HAND to foot.' Kelsal circled Mintah, her four accomplices and six of the crew jangling leg and wrist irons. As though to undo his steps or make a new circle, he headed in the reverse direction. His look of concentration, brow furrowed, lips pursed, brought a semblance of orderly industry to a scene that was otherwise chaotic. Each of the crewmen had his arms laden with chains or else had them hanging from his shoulders. They handled the implements like dangerous pets, loved and cared for and often exhibited but somehow still capable of unpredictable, lethal behaviour. They complained bitterly to each other and cursed the captain's name for his decision to resume this mad work. Rain on the rusted irons made them bleed. To untangle the chains the crew laid them out side by side in tidy rows. The rust sloughed off the irons. Rust sluiced between the planks, overflowed and spread over the deck, distributed by the rain. The crew attached the irons to the feet and hands of the Africans. Mintah and the men crouched in a sitting position which seemed the most comfortable for all five chained together by hands and feet, except for Mintah on one end of the line and a man on the other both of whom had one arm and leg free.

Captain Cunningham took up his position in the shelter afforded by the quarterdeck under his covering of canvas. He hugged his ledger to his chest with his arms half folded. The major part of a sneer was flicked at the overcast heavens and then the remainder of it pitched at the group of slaves decorating his deck. He nodded in a half-smile to Kelsal, who proceeded to open the hatch assisted by three of the crew. Another sneer was quickly loaded around his mouth and aimed at the slaves. Mintah and the men wavered between returning the captain's gaze and checking the hatch for the first sign of who would be brought out of the hold. They were poised for a leap together or so it seemed as they leaned forward to compensate for the ship's list due to the winds. Mintah laid her palms flat on the deck. The wood was rough and its grain barely discernible under a thick sheet of water. Where each plank met another there was a groove filled with wax, tar, dirt, and now water using it as a path to somewhere. The grooves across the deck looked like lines, but the writing could not be read though it was there in that history of dirt and dust, in the wood worn by footsteps and chipped and scratched by the passage of barrels and bags and boxes and the etchings of salt.

Kelsal was the first to come up from the hold, backwards, glancing behind him to check his progress. He appeared to be held captive and ordered by some unseen assailant pointing a weapon at him to march backwards keeping his hands in clear view in front of him. As he emerged into the rain Mintah and the others could see that he held two black, bony arms which were quickly speckled to an ebony sheen by rain. The man's head fell forward between his arms. His legs were carried by one of the crewmen and two others rushed to take an arm and a leg and so ease Kelsal's burden and the struggle of the crewman. Kelsal glanced at the captain, who gave him the thumbs-up, then looked towards the side. He and the men took small steps which jerked the sick slave to the left and right and made his head wobble. His mouth fell open to the rain. Rain glossed the man's lips and collected on his tongue and palate, and although his mouth remained ajar Mintah and the others saw how his throat moved up and down for more of that rain. His first drink of the day seemed to revive him. The gulping of his throat wanted more rain, faster than the clouds could release it. If his throat was to be believed, the rain, in sufficient quantity, was capable of animating the rest of his body. Rain in him would allow him to shake off the grip of those men and stand upright.

Mintah and the four men began to shout at Kelsal and the captain, pulling in opposite directions to each other.

'Kelsal! He's still alive! Please!'

Mintah stretched out her left arm towards Kelsal as far as the chain connected to her left foot allowed. Kelsal paused and without turning his body looked around at her. His narrowed eyes and frown had none of the disconcerting effects on Mintah that they had on others. This impressed him.

'He's as good as dead.' Kelsal continued to the side. With his three helpers, Kelsal positioned the upper half of the man on the side of the ship as if helping a drunk friend to sober up in the sea air or vomit into the sea, then they hoisted the lower half of his body up and the man disappeared overboard. Captain Cunningham marked a stroke in his ledger.

Another man was passed up the hatch and hauled out of it. He was too weak to stand. His way of struggling was to tuck his feet and arms into his body. If he had had a shell on his back his tucked hands and feet, his shortened neck and bunched shoulders would have vanished under it. The crew pulled him to the side. He turned his head towards Mintah and mouthed something she did not hear. She asked the man next to her if he had heard what was said, but he shook his head and looked down at the deck. Mintah inclined her ear towards the man for him to repeat himself, but he was already near the side and was lifted by four crewmen and launched at the sea. His arms and legs retracted into his body when the men released him so that he seemed like a compact bundle spinning out of sight.

Kelsal walked over to Mintah and crouched down beside her and said, 'He muttered Tunde; something Tunde.' Then he rejoined the others at the hatch to receive a woman who was being passed up in chains. Mintah watched the captain scratch in his book. A member of the crew used his club to prod the ribs of a couple of the men chained with Mintah in an effort to settle them. Each moved in a different direction without coordinating his movements with the man next to him, and so they pulled against each other. The intention wasn't to go anywhere, their chains militated against that. They moved because watching in their state of confinement was too much to bear without doing and saying something, however futile.

In answer to the captain's querying look at the woman's fetters, Kelsal shouted, 'She is biting and kicking, Captain.'

'Do what you must, First Mate.'

Kelsal returned to his work. Both the second mate and the boatswain were below deck helping the crew to select the sick and separate them from the others. The sick men and women were pushed up the steps towards the hatch where Kelsal and the crew would grab them and haul them up.

Over the noise of the wind and the rain and the sea came the cries from below. Not just cries for a mother, father, brother or sister from the children, but from the men and women angry shouts and howls, accusations and curses, and they used their chains to bang on the deck as if those planks were the heads of the crew. Most of the women had to be restrained in a corner with a whip and with clubs to allow the sick to be dragged from among them. Those who struggled at the hatch were bound then passed through it. Rain pelted them. They were lashed by the wind. The sea lifted into the air and dived at the ship for the next man, woman or child to be dumped into it. Captain Cunningham made stroke after stroke in his ledger; in his long black cloak, his elaborate hat and with his attention trained on his book, pen like a wand in his hand, he resembled a magician whose intention it was to bring streaming off the page every stroke that he'd recorded of these people dumped into the sea, all of those lost in this expansive burial ground into which they'd been thrown alive by his command, given up for dead, murdered, every man, woman and child, to bring them back with a bang and a puff of smoke, back before everyone's eyes, without a hair out of place, unshackled, smiling and in perfect health.

Mintah looked at a woman whose eyes met hers and blamed her for nothing. Yet to Mintah they seemed to want her to do something, without knowing what, however little. The woman was dragged to the side and lifted up, but she clasped her chained wrists around the neck of a crewman and they had to lower her to the deck again and wrestle her arms free of him.

'Your name! What is your name?' Mintah shouted in the three languages she knew and raised herself up on her knees.

'Why? How will it save me?'

The woman's grip was loosened by the struggle and by another man beating her arms with his club.

'I will remember you! Others will remember you!'

They lifted her above the side, but her passage into the sea was blocked by a sailor. There was a pause to allow him to duck from between the woman and the side.

'I am Ama!'

Ama was held high and flung into the sea. Mintah looked down at her chained hands and feet. She threw her head back and looked at the clouds and screamed. Kelsal came over to her and got down on one knee.

'Ama!' he said and moved away in time to avoid Mintah's lunge at him which toppled the line of four men she was chained to. Her spit caught him full in the face. Kelsal let his head fall back and he felt the rain pebble his eyelids. He brought his right sleeve up and wiped his face, cursed the rain and Mintah and approached the captain. The sea blew over the deck and flaked on his face. He thought of Mintah's foul mouth. Spit from it in his face like the sea. Her words running around in his head, a perpetual sea-sound. His name on her lips, Kelsal, another word for sea, for spit. What he was doing had to stop.

He spoke urgently to the captain. The men watched, unable to hear above the wind and rain. 'Right, men, rest.' Captain Cunningham's order was greeted with sighs of relief from the crew, most of whom slumped down on the deck right where they stood.

They exchanged hard looks and shakes of the head. It was barely afternoon and their day had been ruined. Not by the rain. That was a welcome distraction under the circumstances, cooling them and acting as another impediment to the smooth running of their routine. Nor the high wind, another coolant, which shortened their time at sea and made the most ordinary manoeuvre into an accomplished feat on account of its sudden swirls and gusts in all manner of directions. What irked them was that they were already tired and they hadn't attended to the duties of the ship.

There was a degree of madness to what they were doing. Here they were at sea surrounded with the means to their livelihood, slaves, and they were dumping a portion of them overboard, alive. Only three days ago it had seemed that keeping them alive and healthy was the whole reason for this profitable undertaking. Things had become topsy-turvy. They had been at sea too long. The *Zong* no longer sailed towards land but must have been spun around in the dark, an about-turn while they slept, so that although it maintained the same forward movement, it was in fact describing a huge circle in the middle of the ocean and facing back to front, with a corresponding switch in the minds of all on board from reason to madness.

The captain was the maddest of all. His ledger was his greatest treasure. He held it as if it was filled with gold or precious stones that might spill with the slightest jolt or tilt. He consulted it as though it dictated to him the precise means by which the ship should be run. All in the name of profit. The crew regarded him as the progenitor of all their discontent. A word from him and the madness would end and the ship could return to normal, as far as the subjugation of these slaves could be described as normal. But it had been normal until three days ago, routine, albeit unpleasant, but routine nevertheless. When would that routine be resumed? They wondered if the captain ever intended getting the *Zong* back to order, or whether it would be up to them to restore some semblance of reason or all end up mad.

Kelsal knew their minds. Nothing could be done about the captain without Kelsal's cooperation. The *Zong* would indeed persevere on its backward course and all on it continue to be mad. Soon it would run out of slaves and crew, emptied by madness.

Kelsal and the second mate approached the captain together. This time it was the second mate who asked for permission to express an honest opinion. The captain nodded.

'Captain, this must stop now. The men are at their wits' end.' Kelsal nodded encouragingly at the second mate.

'The men have taken a lot these last three days. This cannot go on.'

'Must. Cannot. I see. Thank you, gentlemen.'

The captain turned to the crew scattered about the deck. He looked up at the clouds, squinted against wind and rain and gritted his teeth.

'Captain, look at the female . . .'

'Yes, Mr Kelsal, I have eyes.'

'She is near to distraction. Who will buy her if she is mad?'

Captain Cunningham looked at Mintah and his eyes widened. He seemed to be noticing her for the first time that day. She was lying on the deck and her head was cupped in the crook of the arm of the young man chained to her, keeping her head just above the rainwater on the deck. Her mouth was open and her body shook but there was no sound of crying. There was too much rain on her face to discern tears.

'Not just her, Captain, others will fall into despair too.'

Kelsal nodded emphatically at this interjection by the

second mate, but the captain did not seem to hear. He stowed his ledger under his cloak and made his way over to Mintah and leaned forward to view her. He said something to her and it appeared to register with her since she stopped shaking and turned her face away from him, even though he stood over her and his body sheltered her from the rain. He saw that she preferred the rain pelting her face to his presence. He raised his eyebrows and turned down his mouth and retreated to the shelter of his piece of canvas. He gripped his ledger under his arm and clapped a couple of times. This had the desired effect of getting the crew to look in his direction. The boatswain, who had stood by silently until now, fished out his whistle from his breast pocket and blew on it as reinforcement. The crew dragged themselves to their feet and shuffled over to the captain. From their demeanour it was clear that the last thing they wanted to hear was another order from him. Kelsal and the second mate nodded encouragingly at them. This gesture ordinarily had the effect of speeding up their actions. But they proceeded in the same reluctant manner, not out of impudence, if their expressions, rather than their movements, were anything to go by, but from a genuine exhaustion, and their vacant stares showed many had retreated into a state of near sleepwalking.

'Crew. We have reached our goal. Twenty-six today. Thank you for your cooperation.'

The captain spun on his heel and dived out of sight to his quarters, through a door quickly opened by the boatswain. Kelsal occupied the vacant spot beneath the tarpaulin.

'Get those five below. Keep them chained together. Eat a good lunch, men, and get some rest. You've earned it. We'll exercise the slaves later.'

Kelsal braced himself for any protest but was met with acquiescence. He proffered a slight conciliatory smile to the men and, assisted by the second mate and several others who seemed refreshed by the news, they pushed and pulled Mintah and the four men into the hold.

'Kelsal! Throw me into the sea! Please, Kelsal. Throw me into the sea! Kelsal!'

Kelsal grimaced as if struck unexpectedly on the back of the neck. For a moment he saw, not Mintah, but the girl who had nursed him at the fort. The fort was not on a map. Not any more. It had been plundered. Yet he had kept it intact in his mind and her with it. Rather than carrying it around inside him, it seemed as if he were conveyed by it, hung on the skeleton of it, so that the girl who had nursed him there somehow cohabited with him in his bones. The burden affected his posture. Made him stoop and made walking difficult. No, he told himself, that was his sea legs, not his past. Mintah was his past. Not his way of walking into his future. The weight was the drag of the sea. He had felt it wading ashore after the shipwreck and when his body had been pinned down in a fever at the fort. The fort had taken the place of the sea in his body, and he wasn't even aware when it had happened or how, except that Mintah had had something to do with it. She had returned into his life like a recurring fever, and the transaction between the sea and the fort over his body had taken place then. Before Mintah's return the fort was behind him. Not ahead of him, anticipating his next step, his next thought, but firmly at his back. Now she had come and reversed things. With Mintah on board the *Zong* had become the fort. He had done what he had done to her because he wanted to be Kelsal again, not the Kelsal she summoned when she called his name, but First Mate Kelsal of the *Zong*. Kelsal stooping as dictated by the low ceilings and narrow gangways of the *Zong*. Kelsal with sea legs and a ship's posture.

Below decks the wind boomed, but without body since it could not be felt any more. Rain on the ship was silenced by thick wood, needing more than fingers to be heard behind the hull and above the sea. Only the sea made the ship sway, and the list to leeward served as a reminder of the wind; a voice with a body. Mintah was chained with the women, and Kelsal made sure his kerchief was secured around her mouth and her arms chained behind her back as well as bolting her chained legs to the deck. She was still throughout. Her flesh had become wood. She looked out of her head to a world that had retreated into the distance. People next to her seemed beyond her reach. Their voices and commands sounded from across a valley where they could not be seen as more than dots or specks on a hillside, and all their individual words were welded into one sound that might pass as a call from any number of the creatures common to valleys. A hand pushed her. She felt a jolt but registered no pain, not a hand on her but a hand she saw that made contact with her body, and she surmised from the hand and the jolt that she had been touched, hit, punched, slapped or simply pushed in some direction required of her by that hand. The dimensions of her body fell away from her. Melted out of her head. With her eyes shut she had no idea where her feet ended and the ship began or air or another's body. The deck she lay on did not feel hard to her or damp or hot. She felt nothing, not even numb. Where she ended and the deck began was something her open eyes could not judge. Her eyes looked out of a place she felt a stranger to and they saw a world that meant nothing to her. She had no place in it.

People moved around her. At one point three faces peered into hers and her eyelids were peeled back and she could hear herself being discussed but only caught a few of the faraway words. Then the faces went away. And she was left. For how long she could not tell. Then the faces returned and she was lifted into a sitting position, a knee in the small of her back kept her upright and her shoulders were held. Fingers prised off her gag and the end of a funnel was eased into her mouth and down her throat. A mouth, a throat. Both were nearby, not across the valley, but she was numb to the movements of both. There was a jolt in her neck. Something that steamed a little, and so must have been warm, was poured down the funnel and into the hold of the throat. Water too. Not the sea. The hold kept out the sea. At last the funnel was pulled away and the mouth and throat made a noise like coughing. That knee braced in her back was withdrawn and she was eased on to the deck on her stomach. The kerchief was left around her neck. Her hands were unshackled. Then she was turned on her right side. The faces, hands and funnel, the knee in her back, all left her alone. The ship stopped in the sea. The sea froze hard as wood. The ship lost its lean to one side. There was no wind to be heard. Mintah was as hard as wood, as still as that sea and as silent. The faces returned along with the funnel and the hands, and the knee in her back. There was the steam once more rising from the funnel. Her throat moved against the rub of that funnel. Out it came and faces and hands and knees left her on her side. Other hands, softer hands, passed along her arms, lifted her into space, splashed water over her and soaped her skin, washed under her arms, her face, her neck, between her legs, and wiped her dry with swift strokes, and laid her softly back on the planks smelling of vinegar. These hands stroked her hair until her eyes watered and rolled back in her head and her tongue fell to the back of her palate and her jaw slackened. And still the hands were there accompanied by voices that were soft and near, uttering a name she knew belonged to the body that was touched, lifted, washed, dried, positioned on its side and stroked to sleep.

Mintah tried to picture the shape of herself on her right side. A plank of wood balanced on its thin side. If she was hit from behind she would fall on to her stomach, if hit in the front then she'd end up on her back. She had a back and a front. Also there was an outside and inside to her. A funnel proved that she had an inside. Hands had lifted her, a knee had kept her upright. She was wood but she was not a part of the deck. She was a loose plank. And she could bend. Halfway down, three-quarters of the way down, this way and that. Bendable wood. Her grain ran which way? Around what secrets? She wondered what her grain looked like. She saw lines. The lines wavered and the next moment seemed to run like liquid and flow along the plank of who she was to herself. A thump in her chest floated into her attention and instead of disappearing again its noise stayed. Her chest too moved out and in. That too stayed. This was living wood. Wood breathing. Her lips touched and parted.

'Mintah,' she said. 'I am Mintah.'

This was her voice. Not the wind nor the sea. Her eyes narrowed and took in a hot, pungent, cramped, noisy place. She recognised it and herself in it. Everything blurred. This was crying. She couldn't help it right now. Wind leaned the ship. Sea made it sway.

'I am Mintah. I was thrown into the sea and the god of wood held out his hand to me and I took it and climbed out of the sea.'

2

Chapter Nine

THE CURIOUS MEMBERS of the public, interested parties, representatives of the two adversarial sides and the sheriff of the court, scraped, shuffled and murmured on to their feet as the clerk of the court announced the entrance of Lord Chief Justice Mansfield. Lord Mansfield straightened his wig and approached his pivotal position anchored high up at the back of the courtroom overlooking everyone. Before he sat he flicked his gown from under him. It fell around his legs and his chair, giving him the appearance of floating above the proceedings. He nodded to the clerk, who passed on the signal to the crowd that they might resume their seats. An unexceptional crowd for what should be a conventional hearing: a party of avaricious investors pitted against a parsimonious insurer. Lord Mansfield was sure he'd be out of the court in time to dine at The King's Head, a cured pheasant, his favourite. The counsel for the investors had stood before him on many occasions. A dour fellow from Halifax with a thick Yorkshire accent, who was prone to axe-like accusations or loquacious summaries as the spirit moved him. Lord Mansfield hoped and prayed that the fellow was predisposed towards the former on this day of days with its promise of a pheasant. He wanted his palate gently stirred and whetted by the morning's deliberations rather than having his stomach's tumultuous acids shaken and flushed to his throat. If he pictured everyone in various stages of being smoke-cured he would surely accelerate events and time itself to that propitious date at The King's Head.

But the details of the case were distasteful to him. Thinking about what he had read in preparation for it threatened to stir those awful acids in his stomach and send them climbing to his throat. He was puzzled by the size of the claim, the sheer scale of the reparations, the terrible numbers involved, and wondered why all men could not approach their holdings with the humanity and common sense which he deployed towards his considerable stock himself. They make you a profit, he thought, so protect them from harm and enhance that profit.

Perhaps this particular statute encouraged abuse. Maybe a man could be so warped by the need to make a profit that any measure was open to him, however despicable and against the basic precepts of sanity. Could it be? He wasn't sure. He would hear the arguments. Certainly everything he'd seen so far pointed to excess, to a use of undue caution on the part of the captain, given his decision to dispose of so many sick slaves. Yet who could really judge such a man unless he too were out there in the middle of nowhere, at sea for weeks at a time confined on a ship? What becomes of necessity to the mind of such a man? The law was clear. Any ruling based on it would have to be in favour of those guided by its strictures.

The counsel for the investors carried himself as if he had a watertight case and Lord Mansfield's ruling were merely a formality. There was the captain's ledger, evidence in black and white and a clause to match concerning the action. How could the insurers not concede defeat? Yet here the investors were before the highest law in the land having to argue their case for compensation with an array of witnesses on their side, a captain, a first mate, second mate and boatswain, even a cook in the wings if needed.

Lord Mansfield hammered twice on the oak desk with his gavel. 'As you know, gentlemen, this is not a criminal trial. It is a hearing. Nevertheless, any judgment passed by me in this court is binding under English law. I will hear the evidence for and against the insurers and investors, then I will give my ruling in favour of one or the other. This judgment of mine, is, of course, subject to the usual process of appeal. Any questions?' Both counsels looked at each other briefly then at Lord Mansfield, and shook their heads.

As counsel for the insurers, Mr Wilkes had completed his calculation of the *Zong*'s claim. The mathematics displeased him. For each head £39. At 131 heads that was a staggering £5,109! Mathematics notwithstanding, there was something not quite right about the circumstances of the claim. Inconsistencies abounded. He could smell deceit but proving it would be tricky. Mr Wilkes stood up and clasped his long black gown that disguised his tall bony frame, fleshing it out with fabric. He jutted his thin face with its sharp cheekbones and pointed chin and nose towards Lord Mansfield and launched into his opening speech.

'I intend to show that the actions of the captain of the *Zong* were unnecessary and therefore my client is not liable for the damages claimed by the ship's investors.'

Lord Mansfield felt irritable; he could feel – from what had just been said – a lengthy argument was about to be launched at him. Indeed, the insurers would have to prove it. Doubting the necessity for the action is one thing, proving it is quite another. How could they possibly know anything about necessity? Stuck in the coffee houses of London with their noses buried in gossip columns or else in cups. He leaned into his high-backed chair as Mr Wilkes continued.

'The captain's ledger records a continuation in the spread of infection among the sick. They certainly exhibited symptoms, but they had more fight in them than sickness. How else would the captain explain having to bind and fetter them in order to dispose of them? My client should not pay, because it is abundantly clear that the sick stock were not so sick after all since many of them had to be restrained. Who is to say they would not have recovered with a little patience and care? But what does the captain do? He orders the dumping of a third of his stock overboard. Where's the reason in that? How could such a base act be necessary? It is the captain who should pay for his actions, not my client. He should be on trial here for the wanton killing of good slaves. One hundred and thirty-one of them. Not one, nor a few, nor several, but a multitude. Their lives were squandered. They could have been productive slave men, women and children today had the captain made their well-being his priority and not just a decent profit at the expense of my client; not a fairly won profit from a gentlemanly endeavour, but a profit wrung from a crude interpretation of the law. A law intended to protect ships like the *Zong* from disaster.

'A just ruling would throw out this claim for seeking to exploit the law. What does that law say? It states quite categorically that any measure deemed necessary by the captain can be taken to protect his stock from further loss or damage. It must be admitted that this measure was *extreme*. Not at all necessary. And indecent. With the consent of his senior crew and over three days the captain proceeded to dump 131 living slaves into the sea. How could it have been necessary to dispose of so many slaves? It is necessary if, like the captain, one puts profit above everything else. Above the care of stock. Above whatever eventual profit they might bring. This pursuit of a profit by the captain may appear to have served his investors. At first glance one might think it was a good profit to have made under the circumstances.

'Such an assessment would be wrong. It will never be known how many slaves might have recovered from their ailments and gone on to fetch a decent profit at auction. How many men, women and children might have lived or even died from their symptoms, will never be known. Why should this be so? Because the law allows it. And because the captain decided to invoke that law for his own gain and *not* out of necessity as the law maintains. A responsible owner entrusted with such valuable stock would have done everything in his power to preserve them. He would not have disposed of a third of them. The action itself is so drastic it clearly indicates a concern not for the preservation of stock but of profiteering from the law.

'In rejecting this claim the court would be signalling to all those prospective captains who might take this case as a lesson to guide their own actions under duress, that such actions will not be rewarded by a court. The law was not created to be abused. Necessary measures towards the preservation of stock do not include its decimation. How can it? A ruling in favour of the investors would grant permission to every captain to use these extreme measures if his stock were threatened with sickness instead of taking action to see that they are returned to health. This would turn the trade into a use of stock in the most barbaric way where their deaths in great numbers would not matter and all that would govern their conveyance from Africa to the plantations in the Indies or America would be profit.

'As it stands it is only profitable and worthwhile as a venture if slaves arrive at auction in a reasonable condition. If they could be disposed of and still reap a profit for the captain and investors then there would be no incentive to care for them in the first place. Every little sign of sickness would be taken as a cue for throwing slaves into the sea and claiming the insurance. What should be taken only as a last measure becomes a compulsion. And when necessity becomes a compulsion any measure of cruelty is justified.

'Of course, the captain and his crew are guilty of a greater crime than profiteering. They have done a most inhuman thing. Africans are categorised as stock, but it has long been recognised by civilised people that they are only labelled so for their conveyance from Africa to the plantations and not because they are actually equal to animals. English society is replete with examples of Africans who conduct themselves in a civilised manner.'

Mr Wilkes was interrupted by loud laughter from everyone in the court. Lord Mansfield wiped the smile off his own face and with two swift strokes of his gavel restored an uneasy quiet. Mr Wilkes turned his head away from Lord Mansfield towards the public gallery. His grip on his gown tightened. He leaned forward as if to take the members of the public into his confidence.

'What does it mean to have dominion over stock? Does it mean doing whatever we deem necessary for their well-being? Yes, it does. And what guides our actions? Christian principles. Where is the Christianity in this decision by Captain Cunningham to treat his stock in this way? What was he guided by if not a belief in God and Christ? There can only be one answer to this – profit. Profit at the expense of his humanity. Profit at the expense of Christian precepts. Profit regardless of the suffering and destruction of those entrusted to his care.'

Mr Wilkes kept his pointed face aimed at the public gallery in response to the many expressions of assent to his argument that came from it. Then he trained his gaze on Lord Mansfield and bowed his head to indicate that he was finished for the time being. Lord Mansfield shifted in his seat and scratched his left temple very slowly while staring impassively at Mr Wilkes. Once Mr Wilkes had settled in his chair, Lord Mansfield nodded to the counsel for the investors to proceed. He was relying on the Yorkshireman to re-establish the authority of the evidence of the captain's ledger in the courtroom.

Mr Drummond, the counsel for the investors, rose from his chair and despite his bulky frame stepped lithely round his desk to occupy the space just vacated by his counterpart, in front of Lord Mansfield's high seat. Mr Drummond, despite his accent, spoke poetry to Lord Mansfield's ears the moment he began to present his argument.

'My lord, my clients have the law on their side. The captain and his crew, acting on behalf of my clients, acted within that law. Slaves are stock. Let us say that a man has a stable of horses. They are valuable to him. Does he not feed them, groom them, exercise them to the best of his ability? What does he do if a disease threatens to destroy his stock? Does he not perform the same care by removing from among his holdings contaminated stock in order to preserve the rest? This is what the captain and crew did when they removed those sick slaves from the *Zong*. The sick – if retained

– ran the risk of contaminating the remainder of the stock. As a result evasive measures were set in motion. Then there was the fact of dwindling supplies. Why feed slaves who were destined to die anyway? Rationing too had to commence two days after the dumpings in order to preserve stocks of water. All this was there in the ledger, every fact and act scrupulously recorded for just such an eventuality as this: its disputation by insurers whose sole wish always seems to be that they should benefit from a venture and never have to suffer the consequences if their speculation went awry. In the case of the *Zong*, things regrettably went wrong and rather than sink even deeper into disaster the captain set in motion certain measures that curtailed that disaster, contained it, reversed it. He should be commended for his actions rather than have them disputed in a court of law merely because the insurers have a distaste for meeting the dictates of their cavalier underwritings. But let us hear from the men who were there. Let experience speak for itself.'

Mr Drummond gestured towards the captain and crew, bowed to Lord Mansfield and returned to his seat. Lord Mansfield fought to stop his head from nodding its assent. Yet assent was what he felt, and felt hugely: if he had invested in the cargo of that ship he too would have wanted some reasonable measure to be taken to safeguard his investment. The public gallery was quiet, not liking the message but finding themselves persuaded by the man. Simon tried to be inconspicuous among them. He sat forward and shook his head vigorously, blinked back frustrated tears and squeezed the book he was holding to his chest.

First Mate Kelsal fixed his most intense frown on his brow when called to the witnesss box to take the oath and testify. He began uncertainly, muttering to himself almost, and had to pause to clear his throat.

'My lord, I am first mate on the *Zong*. I assumed responsibility for the smooth running of the ship whenever the captain was below deck. Everything happened as Mr Drummond has explained it. Orders were followed during those three days, as they had always been followed, because they came from a trusted, superior source. The captain's estimation of the sick had been accurate. I know how hard it is to look at an African and know his condition. An African's skin betrays nothing of his debilitated state. Hit an African and there is no evidence of the abuse on the body, unless of course the skin is pierced. A sick African only shows ill-health in his eyes. I noticed the dull eyes of the sick on the *Zong*. Like a light about to die, a small puff of wind was all that was required to put it out.

'I know Africans. I lived among them a long time ago. My ship was blown off course in a gale one night and it hit a sandbar far up the coast and took on water and listed to starboard so acutely the crew were forced to abandon ship and swim ashore. In the dark they scattered along the coast, and those who disappeared may have swum in the wrong direction out to sea. I awoke to find myself lying in the sand. I wandered along the coast for many hours then finally turned inland and came to the Danish fort which was full of Africans and missionaries of all nationalities. I was told later that a fever had gripped me and held me in its vice for three weeks. When I recovered I was made to promise I would work for as many weeks around the mission before leaving. Building work was assigned to me, or work supervising Africans. After one day I took what supplies I needed for a long journey, mostly food, and left unobserved, but only got two miles away before

I fell to the ground with the same fever that had flared up again. I was brought back to the mission and cared for once more, and upon recovery sentenced to twice the length of labour as before for stealing provisions and other property belonging to the mission, and this time was watched closely. I was made to build and to cut wood under strict supervision by Africans who had converted to Christianity and who worked around the mission for free and were therefore trusted to come and go as they pleased. Africans chided me for working too slow or not at all and for my insolence. I was in the charge of these men and they dealt with me as they saw fit.

'I earned my freedom and left the mission on good terms with everyone. While on the coast waiting to join an English ship, I heard the news that the mission had been attacked by the Dutch and pillaged and that the Africans had fled into the bush. It was a good place. It acquainted me with the ways of Africans. I saw Africans when they were not slaves.

'The three days of disposals were entirely necessary. Each of those Africans looked to be on the verge of death. They would have died in a few days anyway, after they had depleted valuable supplies. The ship had lost seven of the crew and the ship's doctor. Everyone worried that he would be next. Something drastic had to be done to arrest the whole drift into disease and death. And without the expertise of the ship's doctor what could the captain do but act to preserve the rest of us?

'At first, we hesitated. We had not come across this situation before. During the three days there were doubts among the crew. We found the task, however necessary, distasteful in the extreme. We are men. There had to be the usual grumblings of men. A sailor would not be a sailor if he were happy and willing in any task assigned to him. It is sailors' stock in trade to grumble at orders among themselves and to complain incessantly during the obeying of those orders in the hope that they will be cancelled. But carried out they were. And to the letter. And when it was done, it was done.

'I was a bad prisoner when I was held at that fort, but I am a good sailor. And if the captain is to be believed I was the best first mate he had ever had. His orders were absolutely necessary. What we did had to be done to save the *Zong*. We are here thanks to the captain and a law that allows us to act for the good of everyone. I did everything I could to make sure every slave that was discarded qualified for the part.'

Kelsal left the witness box to nods of approval from the captain and crew and from most of the gallery. Even Lord Mansfield seemed to nod in recognition of the truth. But Kelsal looked dissatisfied, and the invisible burden that he carried on his shoulders seemed to wear him down. His stoop seemed worse as a result of his testimony. Captain Cunningham, the boatswain and the second mate patted him on the back. They were all smiles.

The counsel for the investors bounced out of his seat to take up his position before Lord Mansfield. His accent was no longer audible to Lord Mansfield's ears.

'Mr Kelsal's expert and trusted words should be enough to win this case for my clients. From a medical point of view it is common knowledge that infection is best contained by isolation. What was the captain to do on a ship of limited capacity? Should he abandon his ship to disease? His only course of action was to dump the sick overboard. In doing so he preserved the health of his crew and the remainder of the stock. His actions are to be commended by the court, not doubted. What do the insurers doubt? Their counsel says the necessity of the captain's actions. What can a landlubber lawyer know about necessity on the high seas?'

Lord Mansfield thought this an excellent question. Characteristically blunt and cutting. Keep that up and I'll be early for lunch. A pleasant pheasant. He liked the two words together. Who else was there? The boatswain stepped forward. He smiled briefly at Lord Mansfield and then at the public gallery, where he spotted a familiar face and looked again, more intently this time. It took him a moment to register who it was. Even then he was puzzled to see Simon. He gestured to Cook to look and would have said something had Mr Drummond not coughed and nodded at him to get on with his testimony. Cook and the rest of the crew turned and looked up at the gallery to see what the boatswain was trying to tell them, but seeing nothing out of the ordinary they returned their unwavering attention to him. The boatswain planted his bow-legs facing Lord Mansfield and clasped his hands behind his back. He would speak his mind. He believed that Captain Cunningham took charge of the *Zong* during a crisis and averted certain disaster by his actions. As boatswain, he was more than willing to carry out the captain's orders because he was afraid of what would happen if nothing was done to stop the disease and death. Not one man on that vessel took pleasure in the work that was asked of him. Not one. The work made everyone miserable. But it was necessary work. The voyage was jeopardised, something had to be done. Everyone knew that. The insurers refuse to part with the insurance for the very thing the investors paid them to cover.

Had the captain done nothing the *Zong* would this moment still be on the high seas operated by ghosts with a stock of ghosts. He was certain of that. The sick stock in the hold were each day adding to their numbers as more slaves fell ill. Many of the slaves who were not afflicted begged the crew to do something to save them from the same fate.

They had got lost at sea. Weeks had been added to the voyage. Food and water would soon be rationed. How were they to care for so many sick without a doctor and with a depleted crew? There were barely sufficient hands to operate the ship. Some days the wrong sails stayed up because there wasn't a man to bring them in. The rigging became a tangled mass of knots like a head of hair that had been left uncombed for a long time.

'Captain Cunningham saw that the ship was slowly sinking into the sea with the sick. He made us see how dumping the sick before they died on us and infected the entire ship would be a merciful thing. I was convinced there was no other course. My mind is unchanged. If anything, the more I think on it the more convinced I am that the captain is a hero. The sea would have claimed us all. Thank you, my lord, for this chance to set the record straight.'

The boatswain bowed and stepped down from the witness box. Lord Mansfield nodded thoughtfully but inclined his head towards the second mate. He had to maintain some semblance of impartiality. The second mate moved briskly to the witness box, to encouraging looks from the captain and crew and Mr Drummond. He leaned on the handrail to keep his hands from shaking. A light sweat beaded his upper lip. He wanted to crack his fingers one by one until he'd gone through all ten just to calm himself, but the attention focused on him forced him to hurry.

'First Mate Kelsal speaks for me when he says what he says. So does the boatswain. I am a simple man. My ways are simple. I got where I got high up the ranks because of my speed at picking up things. I do what I'm told. I follow orders to the letter. A captain is a captain, and a second mate is a second mate. One gives the orders, the other carries them out, and that's that. No ifs or buts. No maybes or perhaps. Just do as you're told. And do it to the best of your ability. No half-measures. No half-heartedness. Throw yourself into it. That's what I was taught. I got that without knowing how to read or write. Just by looking and learning.

'When the good captain said what had to be done, I'll be frank I was shocked. But I did it because I thought he wouldn't say it if it wasn't necessary. I did it 'cause I thought it wouldn't go on long. There would be a few and then it would be over and forgotten. But it started and it didn't seem to stop. The more we dumped the more there was to dump. The men's arms ached. My arms ached. We hated ourselves for aching and getting that ache by doing what we did; not honest work, not sailors' work, but throwing sick men, women and children overboard. Call them stock, call them pieces of cargo, call them what you will, they was men, women and children. And we was throwing them into the same sea where we committed the bodies of our mates who died from disease, into the sea we sent them into, to the boatswain's whistle and a prayer from the captain and a moment of silence. We complained all right. We didn't want anything to do with it. I thought, "Of all the things you have done in life, Dawson, of all the underhand things, this is the lowest and meanest." True, it didn't feel right. But by God it was necessary. There was so much sickness on that ship, there were more sick than healthy. That's how it seemed to us with seven of us gone and the ship's doctor and a bunch of the Africans sick. Something had to be done and quick. What the captain came up with was shocking, but it was quick and it worked. It worked because I am here in front of you now, telling you the tale.

'What I did on the *Zong* wasn't good, but any sailor in my shoes would do the same thing if the orders came from above. Not just from above but from a man like Captain Cunningham. Not a man to arrive at something lightly. It didn't come out of nowhere, it didn't just leap out of his mouth. It had a reason, and that reason had to do with whether we would live or end up in the sea to the tune of the boatswain's whistle and prayer and a song. None of us wanted that. We was ready to do anything to avoid that. But what he asked us to do was just about as far as we was ready to go. To dump them people over the side took muscles and time. Took three days of doing. And by day three we was sick of it. By day three we would have preferred the sea ourselves to another dumping of a poor wretch.

'We let the captain know our minds, and being the man he is he listened and called a stop to it even though more sick was there. He listened to us. To this day I don't know if he thought we had to dump more to get through the situation. He just listened to us and put a stop to the dumpings. Even though it was necessary he stopped it. That's Captain Cunningham. You have to be blind to question the necessity of his actions; looking at the man but seeing nothing that is there before you. You have to have eyes in your head that teach you nothing when they look. Either that, or you can see all right but you can't admit it because you don't want to.'

The second mate released his grip on the handrail, rubbed his hands together and returned to handshakes from the captain, Kelsal and the boatswain. Everyone around Simon in the public gallery murmured that they agreed with the second mate. Simon bowed his head and allowed his hair to fall over his face and hide his tears. He trembled uncontrollably. He looked at the book in his hand. His knuckles were white. Although he willed it he could not steady his hand. Everything he had heard had confirmed what he had to do. Just as he stood up, Lord Mansfield announced a ten-minute recess with a bang of his gavel. Cook waved to him and beckoned him to come down and join them. Simon nodded, but his thoughts were in a different place altogether. He struggled to hold on to them. His lips moved as he reminded himself that he had a book, Mintah's book. She had given it to him when he had offered to buy her her freedom, and she had made him promise that he would make sure people heard about what had happened on the *Zong*, that the book contained everything they needed to know. He believed her but had trusted the court proceedings to bring out the truth without it. Now all he'd heard seemed to describe some other ship, not the one he had been on for more than three months.

Both counsels were consulting their notes when he approached Mr Wilkes. Cook called Simon over to join them, thinking that Simon with his modest intelligence had walked over to the wrong side by mistake. Simon looked at him then back at Mr Wilkes, whose attention he was still trying to get by saying his name quietly and respectfully without success. Cook told the others to watch the simpleton make a fool of himself. They did not understand his meaning. They looked over and saw the lawyer glance up sternly at Simon, who cowered, and they laughed. Then they saw Simon speak to the man and hand over a book which the lawyer inspected carefully. Then he jumped up and shook Simon's hand vigorously. They stopped laughing and asked Mr Drummond what was going on. Mr Drummond looked up from his papers and when he saw the excitement in Mr Wilkes's corner he stood up. Cook called Simon to come over at once. This time he waved his fist at Simon. Mr Wilkes put his arm round Simon's shoulder and walked over to Mr Drummond and politely requested that Mr Drummond should ask his clients to refrain from threatening his witness. Mr Drummond wanted to know what witness, since he thought the next person to speak would be the captain. But Mr Wilkes told him he would soon find out and spun round and pointed his face back to his bench. After a brief flurry of conferring between him and his colleagues they all left their places with Simon in tow and went to see Lord Mansfield in his chambers adjacent to the courtroom.

As people in the public gallery witnessed the worried and puzzled looks exchanged by Kelsal, the second mate, the cook and the boatswain and the excitement with which Mr Wilkes had left the courtroom with the young man who was seated unnoticed among them earlier but who now seemed pivotal to the proceedings, their talk grew loud and animated. Mr Drummond took the captain to one side and asked if there was anything he should be told concerning the assistant to the cook. The captain answered irritably that the question itself was a peculiar one to pose to the captain of a ship. The boy's presence in the courtroom was a mystery, never mind his sudden catapulting into the centre of the proceedings. Mr Drummond turned to the cook. The cook laughed and said he was sure there was some mistake since Simon had nothing to offer the world but his stupidity. Mr Drummond asked Kelsal. Kelsal studied the door behind which Mr Wilkes and the insurers had disappeared with Simon. He shook his head, but said nothing. Mr Drummond took this to mean that Kelsal had nothing to add. He looked at the second mate and the boatswain, both of whom shrugged their shoulders and raised their eyebrows.

It was thirty minutes, rather than the allotted ten, before the door to Lord Mansfield's private room opened and he emerged followed in a single file by Mr Wilkes, the insurer, two aides, then Simon. All rose, then sat down after Lord Mansfield took his seat. Mr Wilkes beckoned Simon to sit next to him, but Simon judged it to be a few chairs too near to the captain and crew. He preferred a seat on the end of the row farthest from them.

Lord Mansfield cast a disappointed look at the captain and crew and addressed the court. 'It seems that new evidence has come to light that may or may not have a bearing on this case. Therefore I will admit it into this hearing, but first I must ask Mr Wilkes for another opening statement, and all the previous witnesses to come forward again and tell the court what they know of a slave woman, one Mintah, who was thrown over the side of the ship for quarrelling with First Mate Kelsal. It appears that she managed to climb back on board and hide for some time before she was discovered. During her time in hiding this Mintah, apparently an educated slave, kept an account of her own which she entrusted to young Simon here. Simon does not wish to speak, and the court has no desire to force him to do so. He maintains that everything that he would say is said ten times better in this slave's book.' Lord Mansfield looked over at the captain and crew and said pointedly, 'Now, gentlemen, in asking you to come to the witness box for a second time to tell the court about your knowledge of this new evidence I must remind you that you are under oath.'

Mr Drummond objected that he had not had a chance to examine this new piece of evidence and would find it hard to refute its claims without prior knowledge of it. But Lord Mansfield, clearly annoyed with Mr Drummond, and suspicious of the crew because they had omitted any reference to the slave woman from their testimonies, overruled him; the sudden appearance of this slave woman's book borne by a simple boy had added complexity and spice to an otherwise bland menu of events. Mr Drummond sat down as if pushed off his feet.

Mr Wilkes stood up with all the points on his face shining. He had fought hard and unconvincingly to make a winning argument for his client until the simple young man had turned up like an answer to his prayers with his story and the slave woman's book. Mr Wilkes held up Mintah's book. 'My lord, Simon Dodds had no idea what was in his possession, but he was convinced it was pertinent to the case. Well, it is pertinent. In it are details that directly contradict what the captain claims in his ledger. Many of those sick slaves put up such an almighty fight it is arguable that they would have recovered with care. According to the slave's account it is clear that at least half of the sick should not have been thrown over the side, and the remainder should have been allowed the dignity of dying in peace before being consigned to the sea. Furthermore, she writes that she knew First Mate Kelsal at the fort, that she nursed him in fact. Yet he makes no mention of her. Is this not strange, my lord?'

Lord Mansfield felt those stomach acids bubble some-what at the restlessness in the public gallery. He eased his gavel down on to his desk and it had the desired effect of silencing the court. He peered at Mr Wilkes, who con-tinued, 'The slave woman's written testimony shows that, far from disease continuing to spread unchecked, there had been a reversal with some slaves actually recovering.

How could dumping overboard be necessary under these conditions? Who could think up these facts but someone who had experienced them? What the slave's account proves is bad management of stock on the part of the captain: a squandering of good stock; their categorisation as bad stock when their status as such was far from proved, including the fact that the slave herself was thrown overboard.

'This is the testimony of one who survived disposal into the sea. Were she indeed sick she would not have been able to climb out of the sea and back up the side to conceal herself on board. How many others like her in good condition were simply unable to seize hold of a rope in time and so were left swimming in the sea until they drowned from exhaustion?' Mr Wilkes placed the book on the desk in front of Simon and walked towards Kelsal, whose eye he caught as if what he had to say next was meant specifically for him. 'How do we know this? We know when a child has to be chased around the deck to be captured and then thrown into the sea. Where is the life-threatening sickness in that child if it can run? And where is the necessity in the decision to dispose of her? Her health or otherwise was not the main concern of the captain. He simply saw her as another item to be disposed of in order to enhance his profit made from a claim against my client. Why should my client pay such a man for these actions? Where is the necessity in them? It would be unjust to reward such behaviour.'

Mr Wilkes picked up Mintah's book again and waved it at the captain and crew and at the public gallery. Then he settled his gaze on Mr Drummond, and his pointed nose, cheekbones and chin seemed to grow sharper. 'In his introductory remarks my esteemed colleague equated the care of slaves with that of horses. My reply is that no cargo of horses would have been treated in this way, tied down in order to be dumped into the sea, chased around the deck and caught and then thrown overboard. The health of those horses would have been established beyond a shadow of doubt before any such drastic action was taken. But the law as it stands encourages the unscrupulous to act in this way. Until this law is remedied others will see the captain's drastic measures as necessary because profitable and will come before these courts with future claims. For this reason it is imperative to rule against the *Zong*.' Mr Wilkes slammed Mintah's book down in front of Simon causing Simon to jump in his seat. He bowed at Lord Mansfield and sat down. The insurer grabbed his hand and shook it vigorously. There was a round of applause from the gallery. Lord Mansfield hammered his desk repeatedly to restore order. He waved rapidly at Mr Drummond to begin, but Drummond, instead of offering a rebuttal to Mr Wilkes, requested a few minutes to confer with his clients and the crew of the *Zong* and to examine the book. Lord Mansfield overruled on the grounds that he merely wanted to establish the extent or otherwise of the knowledge of the book and the slave in question among the crew since no mention had been made of it or her in their previous testimonies. Mr Drummond sagged down in his seat and simply waved Kelsal to step forward and offer his testimony.

Kelsal stood up with his head sunk a little into his curved shoulders. His eyes seemed to be reading script written on the floor from the way he looked from left to right but not at anyone. He wasn't sure what to say. Should he tell the court that Mintah made him drink when he was at the fort and delirious with fever? That she was among the young women keeping vigil over him and mopping the sweat from him during his interminable nights when he woke up not knowing his name and had to be told by her, 'Kelsal. Kelsal'? That he had to repeat it to himself until it rang true? Until he began to speak he did not know what he would say.

'My lord, I accept that this Mintah may have remembered me from the fort, but I do not remember her. She was quiet on the *Zong* up to the moment the disposals began. I admit she was not physically sick like the others, but her sanity was questionable, and once insane an African is useless as labour since he does not respond to orders or punishments. The temperament of the mad infects the others into similar disregard for authority. This was her condition when I had her ejected from the ship. In my view her mind was unsuited to a life of servitude. She would forever be a thorn in the side of authority. Her manner would spread dissent among the slaves and disrupt the workings of a plantation.'

Simon jumped to his feet and shouted at Lord Mansfield, 'He is lying m' lord! He is lying!' Lord Mansfield hammered his desk and silenced Simon. The insurer pulled Simon back on to his chair. Lord Mansfield cast a baleful look at Simon and moved his head from side to side as he said, 'Young man, this is a court of law. You must not speak or shout in my court. You have done well to bring us this new evidence, but now you must remain quiet and listen to everyone. Do you understand?'

Simon nodded and apologised several times before he was hushed by Mr Wilkes, who put his finger to his lips and leaned around the insurer to look severely at Simon.

Kelsal continued, 'Believe me, it was absolutely necessary to get rid of her. It is a minor miracle that she managed to scramble back on board. She was unchanged by her experience of the sea. If anything her mad defiance seemed to be intensified. She roused the others into acts of near rebellion. Nothing to commit to paper but behaviour that could be seen as dangerous had the captain not taken decisive action. Luckily, she was pacified. She fetched a good price in Maryland. The Jamaican markets were flooded at that time by a host of ships from Africa. Not so Maryland. She was silent for the remainder of the voyage. She ate, exercised and slept like the others and seemed strong if somewhat withdrawn. She had to be kept in chains like the strongest men, but that helped to fetch a good price at the auction.

'She recorded what she saw or was told from her hiding place on the ship. Whatever she wrote was dictated by her distress at being a slave when she had been free and could read and write. She was not a doctor. She could not run a ship. She would have watched the entire ship die a piece at a time just to escape her future life as a slave.'

Kelsal made a great effort to lift his eyes off the floor and look at Simon, who expected to see the usual terrifying stare that made him try to dodge Kelsal's gaze, but instead he saw nothing remotely frightening and nothing he could name, not sadness, not anger, nothing, just an empty look. Simon wasn't even sure if Kelsal saw him. He felt as if he just happened to be in Kelsal's line of vision. Kelsal spoke with a quieter voice now.

'Any errors in judgement were minute. That child who ran from a sailor did so using the last portion of her strength. The same child had to be carried from below deck. She was in a virtual faint with her sickness. The wind and the rain brought her round for a second and she sprang from the sailor's arms and ran. He soon caught up with her, and she was as still as before and probably dead before she hit the sea.'

Kelsal walked slowly back to his place beside the other crew members. They were less animated and offered sympathetic smiles. He sat down heavily. The gallery was silent.

The boatswain stood up angrily and pushed past Kelsal to get to the witness box. He could barely wait to begin. If he could kick Kelsal he would do it. He thought his speech deplorable. What he wanted to do to that cook's assistant would amount to murder. Producing that book had provided a distraction for the insurers from the main matter facing them: the necessity or otherwise of the captain's order. They should be examining the case according to the law, not wasting their breath on a book with no relevance to the issue of what was best for the stock and the stricken *Zong*. Simon was protected on the *Zong* from all types of abuse from the slaves, who knew his simple mind straight away. He was cared for on the *Zong*. He gained a family where he had none. Look how he repays everyone. This is the thanks we get for taking him off the streets of Liverpool.

The boatswain pinched his eyelids together, creating an intense stare which made Simon duck behind the insurer. And with the look came more thoughts that buried Simon in unconsecrated ground.

'My lord, as boatswain on the *Zong* and friend to the captain, let me declare that these proceedings are shameful and disreputable. I would walk from this court this instant were it not for the fact that a man I admire and know personally is on trial here for doing his duty. I have nothing to add to First Mate Kelsal's words about the slave girl. Her skills were unknown to us, otherwise we would have put her to more profitable use on board ship. She could have helped the captain keep his ledger! Her intentions for the *Zong* were not good ones. She was insolent. We had to search the entire ship for her. The men had to be diverted from matters pertaining to the ship, when we were already short of hands and had little enough time to untangle the rigging, in order to search for her. All her learning only predisposed her towards mischief. I know men who would give their right arm to read and write, but she made little use of it. She kept it secret from everyone. Then she kept this foolish book full of fanciful claims. She was sold in Maryland at a price unlike anything she would have fetched were it known that in addition to her having a good command of English she could read and write as well.'

The boatswain shot a last look at Simon (who again ducked behind the arm of the insurer) before he stepped down from the witness box and resumed his seat. He shook hands with the captain. Lord Mansfield motioned to the second mate that his turn had come to testify. The second mate nodded respectfully and obeyed. He breathed deeply and sighed heavily and began, 'I am not a clever man. I see words on the page and I know some and I don't know some. Second mate. I know that when I see it written. And I can sign my name. But I can't read and write proper like that slave girl can. I got no schooling. Everything I know I learned on the job. What I see I think about, and make up my mind about what it means. I see a woman who is a slave. She insults the first mate in front of all of us. He has to do something or lose the respect the men have for him. He has to do something quick, right there on the spot, right when the insult happens. He can't stop and think, because all the men remember is the insult and the fact that nothing was done about it. They go away with that and nothing else. So First Mate Kelsal has to act fast, and act he does. We dump her too into the sea where we had to surrender our mates with a whistle and a prayer and a song. We dump her and think it's over with, and she turns up again. After we search the ship from top to bottom. Now I hear she not only reads and writes but has left a book behind. I smell a rat. An African female who can speak English, who is thrown overboard and climbs up the side of a sailing ship and to crown it all finds the time to write in her hideaway on board! Not possible. I think she must be able to be in two places at the same time. I look and I see not one woman but a lot of people playing the part of one woman. I see the insurers cooking up the whole plot and trying to pass it off to get away from the fact that something was done that was necessary and they have to pay for it. Call me simple but that's what I see. And I've seen a lot.

'The African female had more than eyes to see. She could read and write. That's a lot to have in this world. She had more than me. Look where it got her. In trouble. Some people can have too much. They don't know what to do with it. They waste what they have. And other people don't have enough.' At this point the boatswain pinned his eyes on Simon. 'They have so little in the first place they don't know what's good for them. They take the little kindness shown them and they throw it back into the face giving it to them. They bite the very hand feeding them. They betray the only friends they have in the world. He knows who I mean. I don't have to call him by name. He got eyes and he got ears. And what little sense God has given him he can use to understand what I mean when I say what I say.'

The second mate was patted by Kelsal, and the captain took both of the second mate's hands into his own and squeezed them. Mr Drummond nodded emphatically. But Mr Wilkes and the insurer frowned and shook their heads.

Murmurings in the public gallery abated once the captain rose to his feet. Lord Mansfield sat back in his chair and folded his arms, knowing the captain's testimony was the last.

Captain Cunningham entered the witness box to speak, but his voice foundered on the sandbar of his emotion and was lost. Words did not fail him, those were available to him in bountiful supply; but what left him speechless was a sudden constriction in his throat and a feeling of a tremendous weight on his chest. He thought himself a man more sinned against than sinning. Perhaps he had done wrong, but what was being done to him there and then in that courtroom was more wrong still. As captain of the *Zong* he had been given a command. Certain laws were in place to help him, he believed, in this governance. Yet there in the court those laws were being denied him. He felt he was now left without the very support that guided his actions in the first place.

According to his reasoning the ship was in jeopardy when it strayed off course in the gales, which was made worse by widespread disease and a threat to vital supplies. During the early part of the voyage he had dreamed of his retirement, planned every aspect of it, sought to bring it about without setbacks. But in all his calculations he had never for a moment allowed for these developments. Not only his trial by insurers trying to evade their responsibility, but the manner of that evasion. Before his present speechlessness had taken hold of him he had intended to open his remarks by saying that the *Zong* had been near to disaster and that what he had done any other captain worth his salt would have done to avert certain catastrophe.

His intention was to point to the fact that all the testimonies vindicated him. Not even the simple lad had

163

uttered a bad word against him. All he had done, in some misguided fit, was hand over a spurious document to the insurers upon which they had based their entire burden of proof of his irresponsibility. He failed to see how they could weigh his ledger and the testimonies of the crew against that slave's ramblings. He would tell them that he knew a ship's workings better than most men knew their wives. That should cause some merriment and lighten the proceedings a little. He'd made the sea his bed, a deck his pillow. Dreaming of the sea more nights than he cared to recall when on land, and crying himself awake for its absence. All for what? These insults.

Death's shadow had engulfed the entire ship. He had seen death reaching out an arm to him. His dreams were of dying, and each day he awoke it was a miracle to him. On the *Zong* he had defied death. He had refused to lie and wait for death to come and take him and everyone on his ship. He had fed death with the sick as if death were a furnace. Death must have thought that the work of claiming the *Zong* was being done by others, that everyone on it was hurrying to death, but in actual fact death was being robbed of the entire crew and stock by being fed only a portion of the latter.

The law was on his side. Of that he was sure. He knew it intimately and allowed any reasoning on his part to be ruled by it and not by the sea that had invaded his innermost dreams, nor by events on the *Zong*. Yet he felt the Almighty intended some lesson for him by this humiliation. He understood from the court's proceedings that a captain was only free to run his ship as he saw fit so long as his actions did not hurt the pockets of certain men in London and Liverpool. Why else was he here before them now?

Why had the honourable Lord Mansfield allowed this

spectacle to run for so long unchecked? While he had made modest gains as a captain in the trade, he had made men like Lord Mansfield very rich. He was being repaid with insults. He was astounded. And though he hadn't intended to, as he got to his feet the entire morning's proceedings had made the blood rush into his neck, tightened his throat, quickened his heart and pressed on his chest, and he wept, unable to open his mouth. Not only wept but could not bring his body under control. Could not open his lips; relax the clenched muscles in his jaw; speak.

Captain Cunningham stood there oblivious to the words of encouragement and consolation from his crew. His right hand covered his eyes, his left gripped the railing around the witness box and steadied him on his feet. His body rocked as if ordered by sea water. He leaned forward to some invisible list in the building that had become a ship for him. These proceedings were the recurring nightmare of the sea as his home, and the land some figment of his mind. He was forced to share the sea with Africans. All the Africans he had ever dumped into the sea, living or dead. All were alive again and crowded round to get at him. The noise they made calling his name was so loud in his head that it became another type of silence.

Captain Cunningham fell to one knee and his crew and Mr Drummond rushed to his side. They helped him from the witness box and back to his seat. His face was buried in his hands. They looked at Lord Mansfield and Mr Wilkes and Simon as if the three had pooled their malice against the captain and induced this trauma. Lord Mansfield stroked his chin and blinked away the water gathering in the rim of his eyes. He motioned distractedly at the counsel for the investors to bring his argument to a close. Mr Drummond peered up at the silent gallery and faced Mr Wilkes and the insurer as he spoke.

'We see here the result of hard work and dedication repaid with malice. Captain Cunningham should be celebrated here today not vilified. Over three days he carried out a careful sorting of sick from healthy. The captain's ledger attests to the fact that he witnessed the disposal of every piece. Under his careful scrutiny and with the direct participation of his most trusted men this action was carried out to good effect. What is being argued by the insurers? Necessity. Who was there from the underwriters to make such an assessment contrary to that of the captain? No one. The captain's judgement in these matters cannot be accepted by them if it results in a profit and rejected if it does not. If he is to be entrusted with a ship and rules to guide him and if he is forced to act in a way that is deemed to be drastic but necessary for the preservation of his ship, then act he must. It is not for the insurers then to pick and choose which action of his they sanction and which they do not condone. There lies impunity. What is fair? To accept the judgement of the captain in this case as in all previous cases. To go by the letter of the law which says this course of action is acceptable where endangered stock are concerned.'

Now Lord Mansfield did nod, and to disguise it he coughed repeatedly and shuffled the papers, spread according to some private design in front of him, into a hasty pile.

The counsel for the investors continued, 'Here is the clause in question, clause 2, section 3 and I quote, "Any necessary action can be taken by the captain concerning livestock if the said action aims at the preservation of said stock." The stock were living, but they posed a danger to the rest and to the crew. Is this not like putting down a rebellion by stock to preserve one's holdings, where similar loss of life results? An insurrection is easily grasped by the insurers. They can readily see that unless the fractious elements are removed by any means available to the captain then the entire venture is in jeopardy. They can see that because they are only persuaded by extremes. Here is a more quiet but none the less dangerous situation: death by the spread of disease. The captain met this danger by executing a systematic disposal of contaminated stock in order to preserve the remainder.'

Lord Mansfield nodded and this time thought nothing of it. Had his slave holdings been in jeopardy he would want this man to defend him in a court of law. He was very able. He made a man think, and thinking always made Lord Mansfield hungry. Speak on, he thought.

'This line of work is not for the faint-hearted. The *Zong* completed its venture albeit with depleted stocks, and with the consent of the insurers it will reap a good profit for the investors. Captain Cunningham is one of the most experienced men in the trade. It is not gentlemanly to doubt him publicly in this way. His honour has been called into question by the insurers for no other reason than that they are reluctant to part with their money.'

Nevertheless the number of slaves disposed of worried Lord Mansfield. He thought 131 pieces too much. He wished he knew more about the female slave who miraculously climbed back on board ship and wrote about it. Then there was the troubling matter of the ten who jumped overboard out of despair, mistaking the whole dumping procedure as some mad act by the captain and crew to empty the ship and therefore taking matters into their own hands. This course of action by the holdings was not uncommon, but he thought their loss regrettable. They were, after all, healthy stock. The insurers were bound to make a meal of this fact, regrettable or not. In his twenty years in court, Lord Mansfield had not presided over a single case concerning stock that was not within the letter of the law. The case of the *Zong* seemed no exception. The burden of proof was surely settled with the circumstances described by the captain and crew, even if their counsel's argument was dispensed with.

'Disaster was averted, without a doubt. The alternative would have been to nurse the sick. How? The ship's doctor had succumbed to disease. And seven of the crew. Had the captain waited there would have been no one left on the *Zong*. Think of the unnecessary suffering that was avoided by this humane action. Instead of watching the sick die a slow and prolonged death, he cut short their suffering by this merciful act and saved the rest and saved invaluable supplies. May I remind the court that emergency rationing ensued only two days later despite all the sick that were dumped. So the ship was threatened not only by disease but with starvation too. The *Zong* docked in Jamaica, where most of the stock were sold, and then sailed to Maryland, where the last of them were auctioned. Between Jamaica and Maryland nothing out of the ordinary occurred.

'It is my contention that this slave's account is a fabrication by the insurers and as such it should not have been admitted as evidence because a slave could not have written it. Think about where those slaves were found. Consider too their condition on board ship. How could a slave have procured writing materials over two days and kept the book from the crew?

'From the captain's ledger it is clear that a thorough search of the ship was carried out and the slave was not found, which leads me to believe she was aided and abetted by the cook's assistant. What does this second account say? Everything the insurers would like to believe. That the ship's holdings were in a good condition and that the dumpings were unnecessary and therefore Captain Cunningham has committed some murderous act. These allegations are dignified by my repetition of them here, but I only do so to point out the ludicrous lengths to which the insurers are prepared to go to avoid meeting their promise.

'This book – penned by a ghost, it seems, since the hand has not been produced here today in this court to prove its authorship – does not dispute any of that. Let us examine the source. A simple-minded young man. Unable to read and write and barely able to count past ten. It raises questions outside the jurisdiction of this court.'

Mr Drummond conceded that there was clearly an intelligence at work in it, but it was not admissible in this case, if only because it argued against the law concerning the status of Africans as stock. The woman thought to be responsible for its authorship was nowhere mentioned in the captain's ledger.

'Are you seriously suggesting that an African female literate in English would be bought by the captain unknowingly and concealed on his ship and he would have no inkling of her presence in a voyage of over ten weeks?' he challenged Mr Wilkes.

The entire court murmured its assent, leaving the counsel for the insurers flustered. Lord Mansfield nodded his approval. He was hungry. Things were settled in his mind, and in his stomach the juices were in a state of readiness.

'What we are seeing with the presentation of this book is an attempt by the insurers to divert attention from the matter at hand, namely their culpability in this case.'

Lord Mansfield agreed. The insurers should of course pay up. There was nothing in this new account that he'd seen to alter that fact of the law regarding the treatment of stock. Why the boy had been persuaded to deliver himself to the wrong side puzzled Lord Mansfield. And with a book of ingenious wit if invented, and all the more remarkable if genuine. It all seemed too fanciful to be a ploy by the insurers. The cruelty or otherwise of the captain's decision was for another court, not his.

'I only mention this other book to show how far the court has strayed from the issue. Let me add, in answer to two points raised by my learned friend acting for the other side, first, that there were disputes on board between the captain and his first mate. The latter did not agree with the necessary action. But the matter was resolved and the first mate cooperated fully with his captain. And second, that the slave's account speaks of incessant rain. It does indeed contradict the captain's decision to start rationing water two days after the end of the disposals. Which are we to believe? The captain's account or the ghost-written musings of a mind prone to invention, it seems, from the stories about the land and the sea?'

Lord Mansfield agreed wholeheartedly even though the tone of the Yorkshireman was reprehensible since it implicitly criticised his decision to allow the second account to be admitted in the court. True enough, the details of it were not for his court to consider, but evidence from all sources had to be heard. The judgment was straightforward in his opinion. These underwriters should pay for the loss of the stock. They were liable for it based on the law as carried out by Captain Cunningham.

Mr Drummond faced the gallery for his conclusion. 'Do not allow a cat to be thrown among the pigeons. This second account is meant to confuse the situation by diverting our attention from the law. Which law did the captain break? None according to English statutes. What is being disputed here? Whether his actions were within the law that describes the treatment of slave stock. We are here today for the express reason of proving the underwriters wrong in their refusal to pay for the losses on the *Zong*. Necessity is a part of the issue, and the captain has proven his actions by his ledger and by the testimony of his crew. What Captain Cunningham did ensured the preservation of the majority of his holdings. Now it is for the insurers to meet their obligation. Captain Cunningham has fulfilled his part of the bargain. He has brought us the *Zong* laden with stock. Not as much as predicted, but more than expected under the circumstances. The investors purchased insurance at a high cost to themselves for this very eventuality: that given certain unforeseen circumstances that might threaten their stock, they would wish to be covered by insurance against such loss or damage. Why now should they be told by those very insurers that their actions were unnecessary just because the result entails an insurance cost? This is not gentlemanly.

'The insurers should be grateful that the extent of their liabilities is so little compared to what they might have been had the captain done nothing. We should question the validity of the insurers' refusal to pay, rather than the integrity of Captain Cunningham.'

The spectators applauded and cheered. Lord Mansfield waited for the noise to abate, savouring it as if the words were his and not the Yorkshireman's. He took his time to tap his gavel three times on his desk and call for quiet in the court. Everyone was well and truly smoked in his mind. Lunch was imminent. He'd sum up in favour of the investors and order the insurers to pay up right away. The means used to preserve the ship's holdings were distasteful to him, but the action was necessary. A pleasant pheasant indeed.

Chapter Ten

S IMON HAD HANDED Mintah's journal to the lawyer
acting for the insurers after he had heard the depo-
sitions of the boatswain and the first and second mates.
All had told a story of slaves too sick to walk unaided.
There was no mention of Mintah nor of the attempt by
her and four other slaves to take over the ship. The two
deaths among the crew that resulted were put down as
accidental. He knew those two men. They were gruff and
surly and rarely had a kind word for him or for the cook
at mealtimes, but they were hard-working sailors. Both
deserved to be remembered for dying on duty, not by
accident but by design. They died at the hands of slaves,
but those hands were twisted by the captain.

Simon remembered the very moment the order was
given and discussed and then carried out. He could feel
the rain, would always associate wind and rain with the
memory. And seeing the work of handling the slaves,
hearing their cries in his sleep, had poisoned the sea he had
dreamed about before ever seeing. His sea had become a
dumping ground for the living. Sea water turned red in his
dreams. He dreamed he was clinging to the highest part
of a mast afraid of having any contact with the sea. He

would have to go back and reclaim it somehow. Separate sea from blood. And be rocked to sleep by the sea.

If those two men deserved to be remembered, then Mintah was most deserving of all. Mintah and the drowned sick and the ten others who had taken it upon themselves to end their lives and had jumped unaided. Simon had known what he had to do with her writings when he had heard the untruths spread by the senior crew. It had become clear to him that he couldn't give the book to the Yorkshireman representing them. When he had approached the lawyer for the insurers Simon could tell from the man's ashen face that what he had to say was the equivalent of showing him proof of the existence of ghosts. The lawyer steadied himself, dropped into a chair, perused the ghost-book in silence and then cackled aloud and summoned his colleagues to look. Simon too had to swear that what he had said was true and that he had come by the book honestly.

When the captain and crew had got wind of Simon's actions everyone concerned had wanted to wring his neck. The boatswain had signalled as much when he ran his index finger across his throat and glared across the court at Simon, sitting in pride of place on the bench with the lawyer for the insurers. Throughout the deliberations he was certain that Mintah's story and that of the other slaves would be told and some justice would come about. After all, they were in an English court of law.

Simon couldn't work out what had gone wrong. Why had the ruling gone in the investors' favour with no mention made of the deaths? He didn't know. He felt sure he had betrayed Mintah. Everyone had been reduced to stock and that was the end of it. Mintah's diary had been dismissed because she was not free but owned as stock. He should not have given up Mintah's memory and that of the other slaves to Mr Wilkes. His entire argument revolved around proving the necessity or otherwise of the captain's actions.

Now he had nothing to show for his trouble. In addition he had to contend with the animosity of the captain, crew and cook. Like Mintah he would have to hide. Find a place frequented by few. Assume a new identity. But who was he apart from Simon? The cook had always told him he had no father and that he had killed his mother at birth. He'd have to invent a past without a ship as his home and Cook as his guide. Everyone had referred to him as simple. He thought of himself as such, as someone incapable of anything but the most basic functions. If that were true how could he hope to be like Mintah? He was doomed. He might as well walk over to the boatswain, hand him a knife and lay his own neck in the man's murderous lap.

It confused him that the word 'necessary' could not be applied to a man, yet if that man was stock then anything could be done to him that was judged 'necessary' by those in charge of him. He thought of himself as a horse in a stable. That was the example that was given by the lawyer for the investors. Whatever was good for the upkeep of that stable could reasonably be carried out by the owner even if it meant the destruction of the horses in it. Again he came back to his question. Why? And once again, the answer he had heard in court presented itself. Because the owner deemed it necessary.

As stock, Mintah and the others had still proven their humanity. They were human yet any necessary thing could be done to them. Mintah's words, her presence in that courtroom, were disqualified because of it. He had failed her. He had come this far only to fail her. Now he had to hide, just like her, from the same men with the same designs on him. He was not stock, but he felt as helpless as a horse dependent upon the munificence of its owner for its well-being.

The cook had told him his mother had given birth to him standing up, that she had dropped him from her body on to his head and he had pulled from her all her vitals, which must have opened like a parasol at her feet causing her to bleed so profusely she had fallen dead where she had stood and he had been left there by everyone out of fear. No one had dared to step in that widening trench of her dissipated life, and he had been silent beside her for an age with her fluid still in his lungs until an old woman as foolish as he would become had taken pity on him and bitten through the cord, holding him upside down to drain and take in air. Then she had swaddled him in rags off her shoulders and he'd been silent throughout, and on account of all that he was irreparably stupid.

He was simple. The cook had called him 'simple' at least once a day during their five years together. And with the name came a blow from anything within reach as if without a word he would be reminded daily of his simplicity. Bruises would remind him of it. When he pressed anywhere on his body with his fingertips and it hurt he'd think nothing of the pain, no word except the one for bruises, for kicks, jabs, shouts, oaths, lashes, prods – 'simple'.

Mintah had taught him to see his body differently. She had stroked his skin. Her touch had invited from his body reactions he did not know were housed in it. Now Mintah was gone, and what she entrusted him with, what had stood for her existence with him, her journal, had come to nothing. And the one word he'd got from all that he'd witnessed during the discussion about the book was 'necessity'. Cook wanted to kill him for it. And the boatswain. The captain too.

As the lawyers gathered with their clients to confer and argue over the fine print of Lord Mansfield's ruling, Simon grabbed the book and ran from Chancery Lane. He jogged towards the docks intent on finding somewhere to hide, not so much himself as Mintah's journal. He passed coffee houses with crowds spilling out of their doors and a sweet aroma of roasted coffee beans and molasses. Tobacco clouded the air and men puffed on pipes, productive as chimneys. Drunks with rum on their breath stumbled into his path or greeted him as though he were a long-lost friend. He had seen the price of every cup of coffee or dram of rum, every spoonful of sugar, each ounce of tobacco. He reckoned, going by this last voyage of the *Zong*, that if the losses of every voyage of a slave ship were counted, for each cup, each spoonful, every ounce of tobacco, an African life had been lost. He could not count but he saw a sea full of Africans. The *Zong* rose and dipped over their bones, and the sound of the sea was the bones cracking, breaking, splintering. As he ran and dodged between people or crossed a road made treacherous by horses and carriages he remembered the deck of the *Zong* and the third day when the slaves were brought up for exercise. Most were despondent. Many had to be force-fed. They were chained in pairs. Two men edged to the side, elbowed aside a crewman armed with a club and leaped over the side. A moment passed when everyone looked at the place where they had stood. The crewman recovered his balance and lashed the nearest slave. Two more lunged at him, but another member of the crew came up beside him and between them they managed to drive back the two men chained together. But on the other side of the ship a group of slaves rushed at the crew and the crew fled leaving a wide opening over the side and Simon saw how each pair of men clambered overboard as if in the sea lay some form of salvation for them, rather than their deaths. Or death became salvation to them; the same death they feared they would be thrown to, they had decided to embrace. Before the crew succeeded in driving the men and women from the opening in the net draped down the ship's side, eight more men had scrambled over. Only after the cannon was fired into the air and pistols aimed over the heads of the slaves were discharged, did the pushing towards the sea stop. The captain ordered the deck cleared right away. His whip and the clubs of his crew did little to induce the Africans to go below. Their bodies seemed numb to the blows. They no longer winced or flinched as each lash or blow connected. What was happening was not being done to them but to people much like themselves. They were simply present in those bodies, unable to feel anything and therefore unflinching. They moved with a great effort as if held back by the wind and their feet dragged in the rain. Captain Cunningham swore at everyone within earshot for the loss of ten healthy slaves.

Simon was glad that the rain blocked out the fact that in the distance more sea would greet him. He turned his back on the sea. The wind's loudness relieved his stomach of its sickness brought on by hearing the sea's attempts to crush the *Zong*. This was a sound he'd treasured before this voyage. He'd slept to it and dreamed whatever its noise determined, cannon, pistols, timber crashing to the ground and his body falling as he watched it from a great height only to be caught and floated by the sea and left unscathed. Now it was red. Now it boiled with the bodies of Africans. They roamed in his sleep and stood before every cannon that fired in it. Shot from those pistols landed in them. The crashing he saw and heard was not of trees that mimicked the sound of the waves against the ship but that of the dead and living Africans dumped overboard, soundless when seen but, in his head, timber, cannon and pistol.

When Simon stopped running it was late afternoon. Land seemed to run out for him. Or else he had run himself into the ground. His feet ached. Breathing hard did nothing to alleviate the burning in his lungs. Land seemed to want to swallow him feet first. His body bore down earthwards, drawn to it, and he did everything to keep himself from lying down without regard for where he was or who might see him. He looked down and his head swam at the stillness under his feet. The way everything was lashed to the ground, trapped on the spot or laboured to move, filled him with a fear that he was in a huge trap that was closing in on him. His body began to sway. He wanted the sea as badly as some drug he'd grown accustomed to that had suddenly been denied him. Land-air left a bitter taste in his mouth. An air too dry and too thin. It lacked the sustenance his body craved. All the sounds around him were sharp and hard. Shoes on cobbles, bells, whistles, pipes, shouts, calls, roars, all seemed to hit the ground and come up off it sharpened and murderous. They deafened him. Left his ears ringing. Threatened to pierce his skin. But he could smell water. He walked round a warehouse covering his ears against the clanking noises, following that smell of water. He squeezed his eyes against the splintered light. His skin began to hurt. Not in any one place but every inch of it. Sound and light pounded his body. It felt as if every blow he had ever suffered was present all at once on him. Land drew him down to it. His legs dragged feet that felt buried in the soil and with each step he was drawn deeper into the ground. He wondered if he should he lie down for a while? But there was that smell of water that had to be near. It pulled him through the ground, the wall of light and noise. He turned the corner and braced himself for a fall. He decided he would not get up. He'd surrender to land, give up on the sea. Allow those noises and that light to form a mound over him and the ground to draw him into it. He would keep his grip on Mintah's book and be buried with it.

Thoughts of the sea, his spoiled sea, brought him more misery. Instead of a gigantic body of breathing salt water, he saw black skin and flesh. The ship's prow parted, not sea, but flesh, cut through it like water, splashed it skywards in fragments like the sea, broke it up in the expectation that it would mend behind, but looking back he saw not sea water mending in a ship's wake but broken bodies, ploughed through. What he faced around that corner was altogether different: light he could take without cringing and sounds he knew could only be made around one element.

The sun was still bright but it had cooled. A welcome breeze flipped off the river. All the commands around him were familiar. And the stench of rotting wood, of old rope in water, and the sea, too far inland to be believed, yet there in all that wood and rope. Simon smiled broadly, inhaled deeply. He stamped his bare feet on the ground, kissed Mintah's book, straightened his back and held his head high in the noise and light as if he'd donned a suit of armour against them. He offered himself as a cook's assistant and general hand to everyone he met until a man who might have shrugged him off like the others, instead looked him over and pointed him towards a ship he said was leaving London at dusk.

For where? He did not catch the name, and when it was repeated to him he did not recognise it and had no idea where it might be on a map. None of that mattered to him. Not now that he had placed his *x* on the roll of a ship whose name he could not read. The name did not mean anything to him. He heard it said a few times, and each time it shone in his mind for a few seconds but soon grew dull and went out of his head. Without the name, without a destination, he still had a ship and soon he would have the sea under him. It was easy. It was simple. He had been true to his name. He heard the boatswain's whistle and felt at home with its piercing sound. Men rushed about him as he busied himself with sacks of supplies. So long as his ground was wooden he'd be happy. The ship's sway and slight lean corrected his view of the world. His body found its usual bracing walk to match the ship and the water. He paused every now and then to watch the Thames as it snaked out of view behind and ahead and, at Woolwich, spread itself out in the light without a seam like a giant pane of glass lying in the ship's path expressly to be shattered by it. By the time the ship reached Gravesend the sun was cold and orange and at its lowest point in the sky and about to be pared away by the horizon. The river was as wide as the sea.

3

Chapter Eleven

I AM MINTAH. They threw me off the *Zong* and into the sea. I should be food for fish now. Or bones on the seabed, my bones adding to a road of bones. But grain emerged from wood, plaited into a rope and offered itself to me, and I gripped it and kept my hold on that grain. I climbed up the side of that ship. In my tired state I'm sure I can't dream, that dreaming would take too much, and I've got nothing left in my body. I'm sure my head is empty in this sleep: some airless room, silent and still with all the furniture in it covered over with sheets, even the pictures on the wall under covers, or no furniture at all, bare walls, and not a living soul in sight. But no. The second my eyes clamp shut the dreams start to run. I see not me but this girl who is just like me. I don't think Mintah, that's me. I think that girl is Mintah. And I see her father holding a chisel in front of him. He carves goodbye out of air. Goodbye, Mintah. Small strokes from left to right. Goodbye. Again and again. Waves. The grain in the air, easy and yielding. His actions small and exact and repetitive. Mintah, goodbye. And the girl following her mother from the compound. Always following her mother. From the well or skirting a field. To the river

183

to beat clothes on stones with wooden paddles, then lay them out on the grass and stones for Time to dry them, using some of that time to bathe and swing the feet in the swift water that's in a hurry to get somewhere. Always following her mother. Her mother's behind bouncing under her tight wrap. Catching glimpses of the mother's pale instep as each heel rises before she steps, and the girl that is me and not me, trying to match the length of her mother's steps but falling short most times, except when she really makes a big effort and hops.

Following her mother the day she left for the mission, leaving her father behind. Her mother glancing back to say, 'Keep up, Mintah.' With a smile and a little concern narrowing her eyes. The girl that is Mintah, who is me and not me, has nothing but her bare hands to return the gifts carved by her father for her as she walks away from him. Her hand in the air shapes goodbyes. Little, imprecise strokes. Some hardly strokes at all. So long, Father. More a way of holding on to goodbye, if only goodbye were not made of air but of something more substantial, like wood. Father, goodbye.

Her hands are empty when she would have them full, this little girl. Holding wood or a chisel. Feeling the grain of wood with her eyes shut to heighten feeling. Seeing behind her, in her past, full hands. Busy hands. Hands making something. Not empty hands. Hands waiting to serve another, doing something not meant for hands. When she looks ahead of her, this girl, she sees two empty hands. Her hands. Following her mother. Not to the river or the well or to or from a field, but towards two empty hands. 'Keep up, Mintah.' And this girl I know hops into her mother's footprints, once, twice, three times, then makes a step of her own that falls short of her mother's next footprint.

'Kelsal!' The little girl is a young woman. There is no difference between us. When I say 'Mintah' in my sleep I see myself as her. I am on a ship. I know by my rocking on my side and by the raised wood of my bed which I have to brace myself against, even in sleep. I shout that name louder than before, 'Kelsal!' My voice has to compete with the wind as it blunts the pointed parts of the ship, and with the sea trying to chop the hull in two, and with the tap-tap-tapping of the rain testing the deck for any signs of weakness. My voice finds a way through all three. 'Kelsal!' The sick men are taken out and not returned. We want to believe for a long time that the sailors have found other quarters for them. We say that this must be what is happening. The sick are being cared for. But the men are taken above deck and not returned. Only the sailors return for more of them. Then they start to take sick women and I know for sure what I did not want to think could be true. Even as I say it with the others none of us truly believe what we say. They are throwing the sick into the sea. We want to see it for ourselves. We want to look at these men as they grab the sick and do this thing. But we fight them and I shout his name, 'Kelsal!'

They come for me with a lantern that cannot burn in this bad air. They hit me in the dark and drag me out. He looks at me and I see a fire in his eyes that makes those eyes strange to me. I see he is confused by my use of his name. He is running wild. I have to stop him. How else than by calling him? They bring me into the rain. I am refreshed by it. The wind wants to peel my skin from my face. Spray from the sea helps it. But the deck is empty and I know for sure where those sick men and women have been put. My hands are empty and useless. All that I have is his name. 'Kelsal!' He knocks me down. Others pin my arms and legs. Then the boatswain stands over me and unbuckles his trousers. The top of the mainmast is in cloud. The ship seems to have risen with the sea to the sky. The ship has caught up with the horizon where sea meets sky. Having caught the horizon it is stuck to it and trapped in both sea and sky. Soon I expect the clouds to take up the entire mainmast and the deck, then the hull, and the *Zong* will be more in the sky than in the sea. As the clouds move so will the *Zong*, and a moment will come when the hull will be dragged clear of the sea and the barnacles will drop astonished from the wood and the sea will drain from the ship and air take the place of water and the sails will be full of cloud.

Kelsal changes his mind about my body. He pushes the boatswain away. What has brought about the change? My dance. My blood in the rain. He has me turned on my stomach and he begins to beat me. Not with his open hands or his fists. He uses a stick. My flesh and bones must pay for my tongue or my blood. This hurt is not for crying. I cry because a dance I hated doing has saved me. The moon rescued me. Blood, my blood, is my saviour. At least this time. I see the deck in water. The grain underwater is clear. The water is running off the deck, along the grain. And with each blow to my body it curves. Now it is spinning. All that grain underwater weaves itself like hair into a rope. In my mind I reach for it and when I grab it the grain goes dark.

I wake up below decks bound and gagged. From the noise around me I know that more of us have been thrown into the sea. The women are surprised to see me back with them. I am not sick. It is not my time. Those who are not chained try to fight off the crew from taking other sick women and children. But they are beaten. The sick are pulled out. They too fight the crew. They are sick and they hope to get well. They do not expect to die this way. Some beg for mercy. Some are quiet. All fight to get away. Not escape. There is no escape. But they fight all the same.

It stops at mealtime. The men are taken up first, then the women and children. Two of the crew untie me and I am allowed to go up too. I walk and shrug off help. I must not be seen as sick. The captain is sheltering in a corner with his ledger. 'Kelsal!' He looks at me and grits his teeth. He comes to me. I tell him I know him from his days as a thief at the mission when he had to work for his freedom and he did not know his name and had to be told who he was time and again. How he said it like a word that was new in the language. Not a name that belonged to him. How he had to grow to like that name again. Not having to look around expecting another person to reply when it was called. Not waiting for it to be called twice before realising it was his name and responding to it with surprise in his voice. To hear it the first time and, without a gap between the name and his thoughts because he inhabited it, be on his way.

The knot on his forehead loosens and his eyes widen. I have seen that look before, at the mission, on the rare occasions when he laughed. Here is the look again without the laugh. And not for long. The surprise passes. Anger sets those features back in place. He needs help to grapple with me. The children are spared. A boy and a girl. Both are sick but neither is near to death. Not by the way they brightened in the air and rain and fought those men. Their sickness will pass if they are given time. They will need encouragement but they will eat, even the cook's apologies for food. What they have seen, children should not see. They will have to be convinced that there is more to live for than what is being shown them on the *Zong*.

187

When those men lay their hands on me I feel a cold wave wash over me. When I shudder I find I cannot move. Their hands are holding me. I fight to get warm and break their grip. As they struggle with me towards the side a bolt of heat and light fills my head and spreads through my body. Each drop of rain sizzles on my skin. The wind fans me and makes me hotter. I want the sea. Those hands cannot hold me much longer. Only the sea can cool me. They fling me at it and I arch into a feet-first dive. I see the sea rush up to meet me. My feet hit it and the hardness I feel is not water but the cold in it. The sea parts and frost rushes up my legs and body and covers my face. I tell myself this is fine. Water has always been a friend. But when I breathe it burns inside like water thrown on a fire and I choke. I come up and swim with my head held clear of the sea. My eyes open and sting and I see how the sea breathes with a life of its own. It is living like me. I look to my right and there is more water until I can't see anything, so I swing my head to the left and I expect the same sea stretched out to the sky to meet my eyes but see wood. Wood packed together in a forest on the sea. Grain buried in that wood for hand to feel and find. The forest is passing me and sways in the wind and the sea as it passes. Either passing or else being passed by the sea and by me swimming backwards with the sea. I look up and the wood is tall and reaches the sky. The sky moves with the ship. Then I know I am being left behind in that sea with no other wood in it. I think I see a ladder in that wood. Each step on that ladder is a join of those trees laid side by side. Then the grain surfaces from the wood, and as I blink sea water and salt from my eyes I see the hand that the grain has plaited itself into offering me help into the forest. The forest wants me though the sea has claimed me. I pull on the rope of the forest and now

I am moving with it through the sea. The sea tightens its cold grip on my body, unwilling to give me up. My body tells me to let go of the rope and surrender to the sea. I look at the fins behind the ship and fancy that I will not feel them eat me because the sea which has taken some feeling from my body will stop all feeling before those fish get to me. My empty hands have something in them. They are filled with purpose. How can I dream of letting go and leaving them empty again? I pull on the rope and haul myself out of the sea and rest against the hull that is rough, hard and beautiful. My toes find the steps in that ladder and grip the rope between them and I climb. The sea slaps me. Wind shakes my body and screams at me that I am a fool to walk back to what I have left and been spared from having to live through or die slowly in. A fool. The sea is my saviour. If I can't see it then I should trust the wind and drop back into the sea. My arms and legs ache with this truth too. But I hold on. I have wood in my hands, under my feet and against my body. Nothing can induce me to let it go and lose it now. I hold on and climb. Not to heaven. Nor into a forest. I realise as I get further from the sea that wood is under my feet and against my body and rope is in my hand. That I have yet to find the true grain of wood anywhere on this ship. That I am back where I left before with nothing in my hands. And nothing to look forward to in these hands. With a past in my head where my hands are full. With a present that keeps them empty. Hands with no future.

Wood all the way up. Grain in the wood. I climbed thinking I might end up back home, convincing myself I was on a ladder carved in that hull leading to my father and his house. I climbed through all that wind rounding off the edges of that ship, seeing as I climbed not a wall upwards, not a ladder into the sky, but a floor to get across, a walk over wood more than a climb, a ride on wood, if I held on and pulled and walked, a ride and a walk and a climb, upwards, forwards, along and around those edges smoothed by wind, since I got turned over and around in that sea and my up and my down both changed and stayed the same, my left became my right and my right became my left, my in and my out exchanged and made room for each other, so I was going up and down at the same time, moving forwards and along on a ladder pointing four ways at once, salt that was on my outside was now on my inside, and I only stopped when I found a quiet place to rest with the wind and the sea all around me, but the wood kept them away from me and hid me from them.

The first thing I do is search that room. Even before I rest. I look into everything. Every bag, trunk, case, drawer, corner, jar. I look for something to eat and to make sure nothing's in that room that can threaten me. I find dry biscuits, rum, water, dried fruit, dried beef, coconuts, oats, rice, wine, canvas, cloth, nails, hammer, and other things I don't have a name for, things without a smell, rough things, things that stretch, crumbly things. Then I see it. A small trunk with 'Captain Cunningham' in big letters. I open it expecting more rum, biscuits and meat but smell nothing, only oldness, mustiness and mildew. I don't wait for my eyes to get used to the dark in that trunk. I just pull up what my hand grabs and I come up with ink, pen, paper.

Mixed in with all this food, most of which I can't eat because it's uncooked, in the middle of it all, is this trunk with a pen, ink and paper. Just the thing I can use. I fall on my back and I laugh. My body shakes till I cry with the pain in my stomach. I stop and I start all over, shaking and crying with that laugh that grips me and won't let me go, so that when I finish, after how long I don't know, I have to sleep. But before I sleep I know what I have to do in that room full of food I can't eat and only one kind of thing I can use. I realise what I have to do with that thing. I go to sleep knowing I have to write everything that happens to me and everyone around me.

Is that why I sleep so deep? Knowing I've found a way to get what I see on this ship out of me? Ink, pen and paper as if in answer to the prayer I never got around to offering. And I laugh because it's as if I have come across a trunk with soil in it. The soil I thought I would never see. There is wood in that trunk, with roots and flowers. I can start to smell the river where I used to beat clothes and bathe and swim. A paw-print from some unknown animal is in that soil. Blades of grass, facing the same way, some with dew on them. A lovely worm. All are offered to me by this find in this trunk.

'Are you living or dead?' The voice is far away. It grows louder. 'Are you dead or living?' My body is shaken. This time not to the rhythm of the sea. There is a hand on my shoulder doing the shaking. I want to open my eyes. Sleep has made them heavy. Even a strange hand on my shoulder shaking me is a comfort. In my head I say I am fine or leave me alone or go away. My lips though do not move. 'Are you dead?' A deep sleep does not protect me against that word. Dead. I hear it. I know what it means to be dead. It is a condition I do not care for. I am only Mintah if I am living. Me, dead? I spring open my eyes and sit up. He jumps back. A machete is raised to the side of his head. There are too many questions on his face for me to know where to begin. He saw me get thrown into the sea, and with his key round his neck he wants to know how I got into a locked room. I want to tell him if I can get out of the sea I can find my way into a room. But I show him my hands are empty and I smile. He looks around confused and lowers the blade.

'Tell me you are a spirit, because if you are not then I forgot to lock the door. Cook will beat me for this. And seeing you made me forget why I came in here. I will be beaten for that too.'

I put my hand on his shoulder and tell him no one will know I am in this room. I tell him how I got back on board. He listens, his eyes and mouth wide.

'Forgetting to lock a door is nothing. It happens to everyone.'

With a little help he soon remembers what he has to fetch for the cook. He promises to bring me food. I am his first big secret. He will keep it, not for me, but to avoid a beating from Cook. His voyage has been measured by these beatings. Not one of his mistakes has gone unpunished. Over the weeks I have wondered whether he would not be better off in chains. At least then he would expect to be beaten for his wrongdoings. But he is paid by the cook and he is beaten daily by him, and he has to convince himself that he is free and that he has something to show for it.

Do I mean to say that a slave who is treated well is better off than someone who is free and treated badly? No. A slave knows, no matter how much kindness he is shown and no matter how comfortable his life, that he is not free to do as he pleases, and knowing this he can never be happy though he may be contented that he is not in a field or receiving lashes. A free person may be beaten and robbed and insulted by his superior for many days, for years even. But there will come a day when he will say enough is enough and lash back or leave. He can do those things and think those things because he is free. He will not be hunted for it and returned to an owner who would then be permitted to do as he pleased with him.

The Danish missionaries came to our village with two messages. That there was one God and that Africans need not be slaves. Many villages had been emptied by the slavers and by chiefs who saw their own people as goods to be sold for profit. The leader of the missionaries argued with a group of village leaders that Africans should work their land and produce the same products for sale to the traders that they would produce as slaves in a foreign land. The land around the villages could be put to this good use. The traders could rent this land or pay the Africans to work it for them. This could happen all along the coast and far inland since slavers travelled many days into the interior to buy and capture slaves. Instead of slaves they would transport what the large plantations grew. But no one would be a slave.

My mother and father heard about the fort where this work would be tried and this one God worshipped. My father wanted the experiment to be tried right there in his village and without the single God as a guide. He believed that the traditional gods would work fine with this new idea. But Mother was persuaded by the missionaries to embrace this one God. She wanted to see Africans remain free, and the one God promised this freedom in this life and in another paradise to be gained after death. The missionaries promised two paradises. One in this life and one in the next. Perhaps my mother could have said no to one paradise, but two she could not resist. Nor could most of the villagers. Father was left behind with a few unbelievers in a deserted village, and it was as if the slavers had indeed come and captured everyone and taken them to the coast to sell them into slavery in a strange land.

At the fort we soon learned how to worship God, to read and write, and work in the fields. The crops were shown to visitors who came from all the slaving nations and the terms were explained by the missionaries. How much a man should be paid, a woman, and a child. How much was to be gained by a harvest if the produce was taken to Europe and America. The missionaries proved that the cost would be less than buying, transporting and keeping slaves and the profits better as a result. They showed too that there was no misery for the African who was paid for his land and for his labour.

But the ships were fitted up for slaves. Industries abounded that had to do not with the produce but with the slaves themselves. These men came and disapproved of the missionaries' experiments with their livelihood. There were threats, and a field was burned more than once. But when the Dutch came with cannons and guns there was nothing to do but run from the fort. Many missionaries died. I ran with Mother into the bushes and we hid there with a small group for two days before slavers captured us. Mother was separated from me when the slavers divided us between them. Her last words were that I should keep my learning a secret since it would get me into trouble. And I should not forget God since he would not forget me. I left her and thought of Father. Father first, then Mother. Both gone.

Kelsal was at the mission before the Dutch attacked it. He left to head farther south where it was thought he would find an English ship. He too saw what the missionaries were doing. A man who worked for pay worked faster and harder and more happily than a man in chains. Kelsal proved this fact. After his first departure and return he had to work out his sentence passed by the missionaries for stealing from them. He was the most miserable man on earth. He wore his misery as if it weighed as much as an elephant. He dragged his feet everywhere. And he complained about everything. The sun, the nature of the work assigned to him, the food, water, the manner of his confinement. Everything. When his time was up everyone was glad to see him released and gone. Except for the children. He was good to tease. His feet were slow, and when he caught a child he pretended to be angry and used his open hand to lash the child a few times about the legs. If a child cried it was out of embarrassment at being caught by a slow and lazy man.

He was always free to leave, but not before he had worked for the fort and repaid a little of the time everyone had devoted to him when he was ill and had to be nursed. The morning his yellow fever subsided, or so he thought, he ran off. Two days later he was found at the perimeter of the grounds crawling on his hands and knees and begging for water and a shoulder to lean on. This second time he was sick for even longer and delirious. I was one of the children who took turns to watch over him and mop his brow and empty his waste and feed him. He opened his eyes and did not know his name or where he was on earth. I had to teach him. 'Kelsal!' I said, 'you are Kelsal.'

'You are Kelsal?'

'No! You! You are Kelsal! I am Mintah!'

'I am Mintah?'

'No! I am Mintah! You are Kelsal!'

'Kelsal?'

'Yes! Kelsal!'

Why was I shouting? Because he seemed to be lost. The fever had knocked the common sense out of him so that I was him, he me.

He was soon on his feet, and repairing buildings around

195

the fort. What a slow worker! He watched me walk past him at a safe distance and he said my name and I said his as if our names did not belong to ourselves, not since we had exchanged them when he was hot and stupid. I tried not to laugh at him or act afraid. He never smiled or spoke to anyone, except to say my name. Then one day he walked out of the fort, without so much as a goodbye, and into my future.

I was in chains the next time I saw him. He had found a ship and he was back on water. He looked happy. I was sure he'd recognise me from the fort, but he hardly seemed to notice me. Only the old, sick and injured interested him. He didn't want them to be brought aboard. As a result the *Zong* waited for two weeks to fill with over four hundred of us. I was below when the ship cast off. Land had to be pictured in my mind. From something solid like a handful of soil to a line at the edge of the sea then birds then nothing but sea. The ship leaned and has never straightened. It swayed and has not stopped.

Am I living or dead? What do I remember about last week, last month, last year? How much can anyone remember? The head cannot retain everything. Why should it? Most of what I do is not worthy of being stored in my head. Or it hurts too much to store it. So I let it go. I wrap it up like the respected dead and release it with a prayer or fling it unceremoniously like the disrespected living into a sea of forgetting. Writing can contain the worst things. So I forget on paper.

I try not to think how many more men, women and children are thrown alive into the sea as I hide. In my sleep I am sinking to the bottom of the sea. My passage to the seabed is not smooth. Fish feed on my body and each bite jolts me awake. But I do not wake. I fight those fish in my sleep. I fight the sea. The sick are around me sinking with me and fighting too.

Simon shakes me awake. He has food for me. I ask him how many more have been thrown into the sea. He says nothing. I hold his arms and shake him and demand an answer. 'Many more, Mintah.' He holds up the bowl to me. I turn my face away. He tells me I must eat or die after all I have done to stay alive. I eat. Salt is sprinkled on the rice and beef and palm oil. He did this for me. There is no taste. I must be crying since he uses a cloth to wipe my face. He dips the cloth in water and washes my face, my neck, my arms. I stop him at my chest and wash myself. He turns his face to the wall. I tell him I have nothing to hide that he has not seen on this ship. Still he looks away. I thank him for the food, soap and water. He shakes his head and says he wishes he could get me off this ship. Before he leaves he hands me a new piece of cloth for me to wrap around my waist. I ask him where he got such nice cloth on this ship. He smiles and says I was made for that cloth, and without answering where he found it he takes away my waste in a pail and leaves me standing looking at myself in that red and yellow cloth.

He does not lock the door. Without thinking I dash out of the storeroom and go to the nearest section, which is where the men are kept. As I walk in the smell I have been spared from for a day made by people cramped into a small space assails my nostrils. The usual bickering and complaints and planning and talk about home and crying over what has been lost or groaning about the pains of the body and the heart, subside. There is quiet for a moment as their eyes take in what their minds cannot accept. This is quickly succeeded by a collective gasp. Then a sudden clamour as those nearest to me try and draw away, and cry out at the sight of a ghost. 'How many men have been thrown into the sea? Not one has returned. How then can a woman? She must be a spirit.' This from an elder who has lost command of his senses but by virtue of his advanced years continues to exercise an influence over the others that he does not deserve. I clap my hands and slap two men nearest to me to show them I am flesh and blood. I tell them how I climbed out of the sea. I move deeper into the hold and touch as many of them as possible and smile and say it is me, Mintah. Some of them hug me and marvel that the sea has not swallowed me. They cheer my strength and luck. They say I am cared for by the gods, not abandoned like the rest of them.

Women crowd at the partition to learn what has stirred up the men. I get as near to it as I can and offer my body for them to touch as I speak.

'I am Mintah. My life was spared from the sea. I grabbed a rope. We must take this ship from these men. They will kill us all if we do nothing. The gods will only help those who help themselves.'

But the elder shouts that I will bring them more pain. Their lives are made worse by each act of rebellion. I should leave them alone. The sick and many of the young men do not agree with him. They say that something has to be done before all of us are thrown into the sea. In the women's quarters two crewmen are shouting at everyone to be quiet. My name is mentioned. I rush out of the men's compartment before they can get to it. A woman in the passageway sees me and covers her face and drops to her knees. She refuses to believe her eyes. As I pass her I pinch her hard on the arm and say my name. Perhaps she will believe her ears and her feelings. She shrieks and scrambles to her feet and disappears towards the women's compartment. I am back in the storeroom.

Footsteps approach. A key turns in the lock and the footsteps depart.

Wind appears to reduce the dimensions of the room. The ship creaks as the walls move towards me. The room is misshapen. Sea water trickles in, intent on breaking down the walls. I am in the sea not on it. My body is dry because I am surrounded by still air. But the walls of the air will soon break if the wind and the sea continue to pound it. Rain adds to the sea and tries to drown the ship since the ship refuses to sink. It seems water is everywhere and the wind is on the side of water. Land cannot be anywhere near this rain and wind and sea. There can be no land left that is not under rain or sea or flattened by wind. The *Zong* will surrender to the sea. Water will take the place of stale air below decks. We will be like fishes in caves under the sea in this sunken ship. Some of us will still be in chains. Others will float off the deck, loosening their grip on it when water has taken the place of air in them.

Land will be a dream then nothing. I live in the past and dream in the future. This present time is nothing to me. My hands are empty so I make nothing in this present. I hide in a room unable to do anything. I am on a ship that is going nowhere. From these decks there is only the sea. And the sea is worse than nothing. The sea is between my past and my future. I float on it in the hope that my life can resume at some point in time. I float in the present. I listen to the rain keeping a false time on wood since nothing comes to pass. The rain stays. Wind intensifies. Sea water hurls itself at the deck even as the sea hurls the ship around in it. I remain between my life that is over and my life to come. The sea keeps me *between* my life. Time runs on the spot, neither backwards nor forwards. The walls of the room threaten to collapse or close in. Always the threat but nothing ever completes itself. Only the sick thrown into the sea are complete. I thought the wood in this ship would stand for land in the absence of land. But the wood is indifferent to me. Grain in the wood has nothing to tell me that can be of any use to me on this ship. The *Zong* dips and rises in the sea without making progress. The horizon is in the same place, the same distance from the ship. The wake is the same length and width. Clouds alter their formations not because the ship is moving but because the clouds are moved by the wind. This is my life without land. Without the land I know.

My body already belongs to the sea. Salt rubs itself all over it. My body belongs to the *Zong*. Wood presses its print wherever I lie. And the captain of the *Zong*. He has me marked in a ledger as his. Kelsal too thinks I belong to him. He tried to stake his claim. The crew know they can do whatever they please with it since it is theirs too before it is mine. My body belongs to everyone but me. I move in it like a thief. I do not belong to it. All this journey it is trying to separate itself from me, to be rid of me once and for all. My body seems to think that if it dies it will kill me, the intruder in it.

I am trying to get it back to land. I know that on land my body will recognise me again as a part of it. The sea has come between my body and me. The *Zong* too. The captain and his crew. They have made me a stranger in my body. My name does not match my body anymore. Where is Mintah? She is somewhere on the sea. Where is Mintah? In a ship on that sea. Where is Mintah? Hiding in a body trapped in a ship lost at sea. The body will give me up to the captain or crew or sea. Unless I get it back to land I will die in it even as it walks with me. I will be dead inside it. My body will set foot on land, and

I will be inside unable to see this land since I will have died inside that body, killed by it, drowned by the sea, marked as dead in the ledger of the captain, assaulted by Kelsal and the crew.

Who is Mintah without her body? Her body is owned by another. Her name is not attached to anything. Her name needs a body to place itself. Just as her body needs land to recognise its name. At the fort I had to teach Kelsal his name after his fever. He repeated it when I said it. His hand came up to my face and covered the left side, then I knew he had learned his name. I took his hand very gently from my face and retreated from his bedside. 'Kelsal,' he was saying to himself as I left the room. He was seeing himself in his name and loving it. My face was warm on one side and still retained the sense of his hand pressed against it. Who is Mintah without her body? She is at sea. She is landless. I am at sea. I have no land. My body is not mine. My name is without a home. I say 'Mintah' and it is lost in the noise of the sea and the wind. My body wants nothing to do with this Mintah. It has more in common with the sea. It is more familiar with the captain's ledger. Kelsal's abuse means more to it than Mintah. It sees the wood in the ship as dead. A hindrance. Wood with no past. No secrets. It sees itself as wood in a ship. No past, nor secrets.

'Mintah?'

'Yes, Simon?'

'You are crying. You were saying your name.'

'I did not hear you and your key. I must have been dreaming.'

'I forgot to lock the door again.'

'I know. But you remembered and came back and locked it, that's good.'

'Why is it good, Mintah, if I forgot to lock it?'

'Because you remembered and you corrected your mistake.'

'But I forgot.'

'A mistake is only bad if it leads to damage of some kind. It is not really a mistake if it is put right before any damage is done.'

'So I made a good mistake?'

'No. You made good your mistake.'

'Why were you saying your name?'

'I am afraid if I don't say it I will be even less than who I am right now.'

'You will always be Mintah to me. Lovely, friendly, beautiful Mintah.' I do not intend to hug him but I do. He looks at me and I stare back at him. He kisses me.

'Don't.'

But he kisses me again and I let him. Then I kiss him back. I kiss him again and again. He keeps saying my name. And I begin to learn it. As we touch and kiss and I hear my name on his lips I see my name attach itself to my body. The ship creaks and sways. Wind whistles around us. The sea hits the ship and breaks. Rain on the deck tells both wind and sea to quieten. Listen to Mintah and Simon. There is breath and salt. Just like us. Listen to Mintah and Simon as they mimic the rain, wind and sea.

His kisses leave me without a body. I am unburdened. I dance in the room, light as air. I feel so pliable I can stream through the eye of the locked door. The lives of the men, women and children in the hold must benefit from this lightness, this bodilessness in the body. Their chains must fall from them and they too must float like me. And all this before land is seen again. All this at sea away from everything. With such lightness I can take the wheel of the *Zong* and swing it until the *Zong* turns around. And any weapon pointed at me will refuse to function. The sick will see this and want this lightness too so badly they will forget they are sick. Their bodies will remember how to hop, skip and jump. They too will be light in their bodies. 'Land,' I will say, 'our land, can be found again if we take the wheel. We are light enough to do it. There is no more to be done to us. Our only course on this sea is to find land and find it as free men, women and children. Come with me and be as light in your bodies. Africa is in our bodies, all our gods and ancestors too, and the land that we carry is light.'

Chapter Twelve

I AM BACK from a parade. A party in the streets of Kingston. The first party of its kind. Back at my usual spot seated on a stool at my front door. I watch people go by with a wave, howdy or good word for everyone. My wood hut is one large room, sun striping the floorboards in places. A curtain separates the bed from the table and two long benches where I eat, sew, read, write, and teach the children on Sundays if it is raining outside. Otherwise they are seated on the grass with the sun to their left or right and I sit on my stool in front of them and the lessons begin. Counting in song, the alphabet tied to animals, multiplication tables in rhyme, spelling contests, places in the world, dates, recipes for certain illnesses, hygiene (I always catch them out with behind the ears, the children always forget to do behind their ears) and the Bible.

'What year is it, children?'

And the children answer together but not quite in unison: 'The year of our Lord 1833.'

'And what are all people this year, children?'

'All the people are free!'

The parade passed my front door. I did not have to go far. There were drums and whistles, flags and trumpets, acrobats and fire-eaters and dancers, everyone was a dancer. I danced along moving my arms a lot and with a little shuffle. Soon I was breathless and had to stop and rest. The parade passed along without me and I stood and watched it wind out of sight, and still I remained rooted to the spot and listened to the drums and singing, catching the kisses and embraces of strangers determined to let me know that they were free and so was I.

But I have always been free, or so it seems. So many years since I was a slave that I've stopped counting. When people I know pass my front door they wave to me or invite me to the square where the dancing will go on for the rest of the day and throughout the night. I have an ache in my side from a beating I took on a ship in another life. It troubles me in the rain and on cold days. Sometimes I sit with that side towards the sun and my dress open so that the sun falls near the troublesome spot. And I try not to think about it. I plan the day or doze leaning against the wall of my hut or watch the people pass.

How long it has taken this day to come! I never thought I would live to see it. I left Maryland because I believed this day was near. Then the years came and went and it never happened. Now it is here, unannounced almost. As if they had to exhaust the supply of slaves in Africa, and the slave ships had to come back empty with only the sea and the wind in the holds. Then slave owners had to grow tired of the responsibility of plantations. While the slaves themselves rebelled, ran away, killed and were killed and came back more disconsolate, more rebellious, more murderous than before.

In Maryland they are still slaves. I shake my head. But I had to leave. I got there and was auctioned to a plantation on which I was told I would die and be buried. I showed them I could work but I could also speak English and read and write. I earned money teaching poor white children. They were eager after they got over their surprise that a slave would be their teacher. I saved and bought myself back for myself. The sea was always near. I tried to ignore it. On dry summer nights I would go to the river that feeds into the sea to watch the phosphorus. I took each glow to be the spirit of a slave thrown into the sea, up river at last, near land at last. After a life at sea and a death there. Their souls sparkled in the fresh water surrounded by land, not sea. They shone with what they had to give but were robbed from giving, with all the years they might have lived and laughed and loved.

I became free and took in sewing and continued to teach children. Black children of free blacks after church on Sunday in what I called my Sunday school. Again I was surrounded by wood, one wooden room sun sliced on the floor, some rain finding its way through that pinged into an enamel bucket which changed its *ping* as it filled to a *pong* then a *sluck* then a muffled *thwack* until listening to it as I lay awake sent me to sleep despite my aches.

I made shapes with wood. Filled my hands with it. Woke and gave shape to whatever I dreamed. Saw my father instructing me in my dreams. Woke and followed his instructions. Sought out the grain in the wood. Found the shapes hidden there. The land showed me its secrets in that wood. My chisel unearthed them. I could almost close my eyes and carve with my father over my shoulder and the run of the grain as my guide.

I checked the port for years hoping that a ship might dock with a cook's assistant. I never got near enough to leave land underfoot. My one condition for this vigil was that land must never be left for water. The sight of the sea could only be borne from land. So I kept dirt under my feet and asked after each ship and sometimes a sailor would raise my hopes with the same name and description, but it was never my Simon.

I left because I had to. My name had got out. 'Mintah' was on men's lips again. And this time I would pay if caught. My wood hut had to be left as if I was going to deliver a dress I had made and would soon return. Friends were abandoned too. I left a lover, who visited on Friday nights and Saturdays, because my name got out. Mintah helps runaways get to the North. On her days away, so the talk went, she takes them to Washington, where another contact looks after them, and she returns by Friday night.

I could have headed north myself. But a South I could get to and bring others from would always be there to tempt me back. The soil I kissed when I first landed was Jamaican. To leave there for the sea again on the Zong made me pull my hair. Maryland said by its trees and flowers and greenery that this could be home too. That land was the same everywhere and the solace offered by it from the sea was the same.

Maryland's wood felt differently in my hand. If it was a sound then it would not be Africa exactly, but even Africa is not Africa exactly. I made the shapes I'd always dreamed of making and some that did not figure in my dreams. People paid me for them. They said the wood I worked resembled water in its curves and twists. The very element I sought to escape rose out of wood shaped by me. Trees became waves. Waves sprouted roots, branches and leaves. My carvings exchanged the two and made the sea home, at least in my head.

I told myself I was going to Jamaica to put slavery behind me once and for all. Another kind of wood in my hands, another soil underfoot. And more sea. The sea that was never very far, shadowing me, would surround me. Sea that I made rise again in wood. Wood plunging like the sea. Grain heading somewhere. To Africa? I ask myself from time to time. To Father and Mother. But the sea between me and Africa would always seem too wide to cross. Not like a river. Not like the goblets I make for visitors as they stand and talk to me, which never fails to impress. They can drink out of them when two hours before they were blocks of wood chosen from a pile in which every block looks the same to eyes that only see blocks of wood in a pile. My visitors do not know what to look for when I ask them to select a block that they like so that I can convert it to a shape they admire. They pick up a piece of wood nearest to their hand, and when I say why did you choose that particular piece they shrug or admit it was the closest. But on further questioning they mention the pattern of the grain or the tone or even the size of the block. If only they could see that what they are laying their hands on is a treasure, that it harbours the past, that it houses the souls of the dead and that the many secrets of the earth are delivered up in it. They have no inkling of any of this so to tell them would mark me as even more peculiar than I must already seem to them: an old woman living alone with this craft and reading and writing at a time when black women have not even one of these skills. And to crown it all a black woman who has been free, and free without the help of a sympathetic master, free in many senses of whites altogether.

My hut is full of the things I have made and couldn't bear to part with. Objects stacked in corners of my hut making it even more cramped. I call my house my hold. It is crowded with pieces of wood. The shape of each piece is pulled from the sea of my mind and has been shaped by water, with water's contours. People say they see a figure of some kind, man, woman or child reaching up out of the depths. They love what I do with wood but cannot keep such a shape in their homes. Such shapes do not quench a thirst. They unsettle a stomach. Fill the eyes with unease. I keep them in my home like guests who will not leave and whom I eventually cannot bear to part with. Often they get dusted by me in a process that is more an examination of each. I turn them over in the light, weighing them up in my palms, and I rub the wood with a cloth as if massaging the grain.

People will gladly take a goblet from me but not these figures, many of them not much bigger than a goblet. They are my goblets. I drink their grain. I drink light from them, the way it shines off head and shoulders and back but in certain places, such as the inside of an arm where it joins the body, or the groove between the shin and calf, is as dark as the sea, or the slave hold of a ship. There are 131 of them. A veritable army. And I have been working on another for months now, between orders for goblets and fruit bowls and trays. I have plans for ten more after that. Then I have promised myself a long rest. Not to leave my hands empty but to relieve them of this project. Maybe turn my mind to some more elaborate goblets, more ornate trays and fruit bowls adorned with wooden fruits that look so real a hand might reach for one to eat it.

For every one thrown to the sea I multiplied by two in Maryland when I acted as guide. As they walked with me or sat in the back of a cart or crossed a river lying in the bottom of a boat covered by canvas and moved farther and farther from slavery with me, and nearer to freedom, I imagined one of those men, women and children rising from the sea into air, their lungs being emptied of water and replaced by air. I saw how the bodies straightened and lightened during the journey to the North. How a chain that cannot be seen or heard is there around the hands, feet and neck and needs to be broken and how that journey with me as guide broke chain after chain.

The sea possesses and never relinquishes. It destroys but does not remember. On land I have fought against forgetting with wood as my guide. Land promised more than this. But land must promise more to get me to work it. Just as wood has promised salvation and kept my hands full through the years. My feet have found a resting place far from home. The sea divides my home. The home I was forced to leave, the new home I had to forge. The sea keeps my hands apart. Wood unites my hands. The sea splits the land. Home from home. Hand from hand. Father from mother. Mother from daughter. Daughter from father. The bones become like coral. Bones washed to a phosphorescence by the sea.

On land I waited to bleed. Months became years. Lovers wanted sons and daughters from me. Not for themselves, they professed, but for me, for someone like me, who should be made into newer shapes of people. But the moon failed as a bribe. I remembered the dances but refused to perform them. Instead I listened to the drums and watched other women dance and saw my lovers go to them with a reluctant expectation of sons and daughters, the one thing I seemed unable to give any man. The sea had taken my blood from me and my ability to bleed. Yet I was surrounded by my progeny. The figures came from me. My hands delivered them. The earth played a part, wood played a part, the wood was veined by its grain and it lives in my hands and fills my life. My progeny is wood. Wood crowds my hut. I sleep surrounded by them. From their shapes they appear to breathe like me. Each has a name, a likely age, and accordingly likes to be placed on the left or right side, on the stomach or back or propped against a wall or free standing. I have decided these things for them. Rather, these things came to me as I gave the wood shape. The wood suggested its name and habits to me as I worked the grain to bring the shape to the surface. They named themselves through me.

Now, today, they are free men, women and children. If I could dance to the drums I would. Any dance. My arms join in the celebration even if my feet are too heavy and my old body harbours too many aches and too much stiffness. A breeze brings drums, laughter, whistles and horns and then takes them away. People come down from the hills around Kingston to get a piece of this freedom, to taste it for themselves and take some back to the hills, valleys and towns flung inland.

Sea and land are joined now in this freedom. To sail from one and walk on the other is the same journey. At least here. And in Maryland before too long. I believe that soon the sea will join Africa and America, though now it divides them, just as it has united Africa and Jamaica. The sea that is slavery will become freedom.

So I had told myself on the *Zong*, tied to four men under canvas on deck in a drumming rain. That night, relived nightly, has become longer than my dreams. Awake in the dream, I never think I am asleep, that it could be a dream. I cherish the heat off the men's bodies. I lean against them. They tell me their names. I mouth them in my sleep. The noise of my talking wakes me. Still I am under canvas on deck chained to four men who took my lead and now face the fate I face. Another's heat comforts me. Names are exchanged. I am awake saying those names and confused by my surroundings. The men tell me this failed deed has made them men again. They thank me and tell me my return from the sea saved them, the sea which sought to scrape my face clean of my features, even though they are chained in the open with their fate in the morning sealed. The heat of my body comforts another. Others lean on me. I am awake and dreaming this. Wind, sea and rain surround me. But I am not alone. I know this by the heat I feel and the gentle pressure from other bodies relying on me for comfort. I came out of the sea for this. These bodies stuck to mine like ticks. My thoughts and theirs running together like syrup.

Dawn strained itself out of the night. The deck of the *Zong* clarified at the base of the jar into which the morning was poured. I drank it with my eyes. Rain on the deck magnified the grain. The grain no longer belonged to wood but had become the rain's sinews revealed by the magic of this first light. Light coiled in the water. And where there was a remnant of dark, in a corner, beneath a shelter or cast as a shadow, light sprang and consumed that dark.

Then the canvas was whisked off me and the morning began to stalk me. Wherever I turned it was there. Rain gave shape to the light. Wind gave it voice. The sea said, 'I am the morning's body and I am hungry.' Men, women and children were brought up and exposed in this light. The sick were pulled out from among them. They cowered from the rain which hurt their skin. Light stung their eyes. Salt too. Sea came over the side and clawed at them.

The captain and his crew began to deliver the sick to the sea. One at a time the sick were grabbed and bound if they fought. The sea was hungry. One at a time they were thrown into it. The sea could not wait. It climbed over the side on to the deck. One at a time the men, women and children disappeared into the music of the sea and the rain and the wind. I asked for mercy, begged the captain, Kelsal, the second mate and the boatswain. I prayed to God. I called on my mother and father. On wood and its grain and the gods hidden there. Kelsal taunted me. The captain peered into my face as if it was his ledger, the night before still crusted in his eyes and laced in his breath. The morning was still hungry. Some of the sick called my name, 'Mintah.' As if my name on their last breath would help them to climb out of the sea as I had done. Mintah. I heard, and cursed the day I got that name. It had become an accusation. A bad omen. A sentence. Death paraded around it. Death was invoked by it. A death at sea. Mintah. By water. Mintah. To appease the hungry morning. Mintah. Into the body of the sea. Looking into my face, the captain searched my name to see how much more it could take.

My name was not mine anymore. It belonged to the sea. I asked the sick their names and heard mine instead. 'Mintah,' they seemed to say. Death. And my name spread among the rest of the men, women and children. They threw themselves at the crew to get at the sea. They would not wait for the sick to run out only to find themselves bound and fettered and dumped overboard. They fought the crew and one after another they jumped into the water. Though some were chained in pairs, they fought and climbed over the side. The captain cursed them and ordered his crew to clear the deck, and the crew beat them back. But not before ten had gone. Not bound. Mintah. Not thrown. Mintah. Jumped. Mintah. Come and get us. Mintah. Here we come. Ready or not. Mintah. Make room for us. Mintah. At the bottom of the sea. Mintah. Our bones adding to a road of bones. Mintah. Our cries in the wind. Our bodies in the sea with a sea-sound falling soundlessly. Mintah. Spears of rain breaking on our bodies and the spears buried with us in the sea. Mintah. Those chained in pairs helping each other over the side. Mintah.

I became dumb, numb, still, stiff, cold, retreated from my name into my body or fled that body as those ten fled that deck into the sea. More death on that deck than in the sea. The shifting sea's deck preferred to the *Zong*. So that I did not recognise my name. So that Mintah would claim me too for the sea. So that when I heard the word I would be there to meet it and be fed to the sea and be consumed by the light and be speared by the rain and have salt in the wind scrape my skin from my face and the sea scrape my face down to the skull. Not to remember that name, nor be associated with it, nor see a body that fits it, nor a past that belongs to it. To empty myself of my name and have sea take its place. Let the sea name me. Be part of the sea's memory. Be speared by the rain. Be scrubbed featureless by salt spray in the wind. Be nobody. Nameless. Less than a nobody by the time the sea is done with me. Beyond light on the seabed. Beyond sound at the bottom of the sea. And movement; except when a current sweeps the floor of the sea and inadvertently combs my hair from my skull and arranges it into a pattern of waves, into a picture of grain sweeping through wood, something caught on the move as if alive and frozen in salt that has become wood for me as much as I have become grain in a sea of wood. My hands empty without my name. And sea taking the shape of my palms, filling them with the sea's name. A sea for a house and its compound. A sea for a village square, for a town and country. Land melted like salt in that sea. Wood scrubbed of its grain. Shifting land: hills, valleys and rock made and remade, with me as a secret buried in it.

How to find myself in that sea. How to rise from it. Have something more than water in my hands. Find a name I can answer to without having to think about it. Find land that will stay under my feet and keep my footprint long enough for me to look back and examine it or for someone else to follow in it. Another's hand runs over my skin and I think hand-on-skin but do not feel. A hand pulls a comb through my hair, but I believe it is the sea and its current. For Mintah is death not life. Mintah inhabits the sea not my body. Mintah has emptied the *Zong* of my people and fed them to the sea. The rain drummed, the wind whistled and cheered and the sea slapped and clapped against the hull. Light fell in spears. Light made the sound of high winds as it fell. Light took on the sea for a body. And the morning was hungry. Hungrier than the night before, the days before. Light took my name. Light made me empty, numb, dumb. Light turned the land into the sea. Into mountains, valleys, rock and wood. And the current of the sea posed as grain. With death as my name. My skull scraped of memory and filled with the sea. Seaweed for hair combed by the current and arranged into waves or grain sweeping through wood.

Who ordered pepper to be daubed on my eyes? Captain Cunningham. Pepper Simon refused to fetch and was put in irons after a whipping from the cook. And who carried out the order and for good measure rubbed more pepper between my legs and pushed some up into my body? The second mate and the boatswain. Who watched and did nothing to stop them? Kelsal. Fire was thrown into me. Tears scalded my face. The flames crawled behind my eyes and into my skull. Fire entered my body. There was no water to put out that fire. I would become ash and cinders. I howled like the wind and tumbled like the sea until I was tied down.

I fell silent. The sea and the wind were mute to my ears. I went still as a sea turned to stone or wood minus its grain. I did not blink. I was the rootless trunk of a tree with leafless limbs. They fed and watered me by forcing a funnel down my throat. I was not my name. I was not my body. I became my own secret, lost somewhere. Time stood still in my veins. Days slid into nights. Light and dark were the same to me. The *Zong* rose and dipped the same or not at all, I couldn't tell the difference. I did not blink. I was fed. I made waste where I lay. It was cleaned from me. I was turned from one side to the other. Days succeeded nights. Time rusted in my joints. Wood left its print on my body. Food and water were forced down me. I was cleaned, stretched and turned. Shadows passed before my eyes but I did not blink. Time became a funnel fed into me. Time turned me from my left to my right side. Time wiped me clean.

A hand ran a comb through my hair and poured rainwater on my eyes, rubbed my skin, washed between my legs. Hands dried me and covered me with palm oil. Mouths whispered my name. I heard the word 'Mintah' and when I mouthed it at first there was no sound, then the wind curled around my tongue and Mintah became a sound made by me, and waves of that name washed over my body until the name was indistinguishable from my body and Mintah woke in that body and a warm sea poured from her eyes.

When they came to feed me with a funnel I took a bowl and swallowed despite a sore throat. I thanked the women for bringing me back from wherever I had been these last two weeks. The news was passed to the men that Mintah was back again, and they celebrated by clanking their chains and banging their fists and feet on the deck and with cheers.

The children sang something with my name in it. The crew came to see what the commotion was all about. They saw me on my feet surrounded by women. Kelsal was told and he told the captain. Both came to see for themselves. They announced land was near. Rations were to be doubled for everyone. The captain said to me, 'Glad to see you have come to your senses.' Before I could say anything in reply he and Kelsal had turned on their heels and left the stinking hold.

But the market in Jamaica was glutted. Some men were sold and a handful of children, but the rest of us had to move on to Maryland. Those who left said they would never forget me. I promised them a similar remembrance. I was counted back on to the *Zong*. I hit the sea and swayed with it. I watched the birds swing away from the ship and head in the right direction, back to land. There was more land to see, and it wasn't the land I had left that I had called home.

I am dozing by the front door of my hut in a sun that acts like a poultice pressed on my body. Children come to me where I am seated with my head leaning against the door frame. They are not the ones I teach. They have come down from the hills. They tell me in my sleep that I am Mintah. That I climbed out of the sea and left my body for dead then returned to it. I ask them where they got such stories and they say from their grandparents. Others come to me. Flowers are put at my feet because my hands are full and there is no more room around my neck for the garlands. I thank them all. They touch me and kiss me and head for the square. Others come to me. They ask if I am the woman from Maryland who helped all those slaves get to the North. Before I answer I want to know who has been spreading these tales about me. They say it is known to everyone. That when I arrived years ago the people who helped me get a passage on the ship to Kingston told everyone that I had helped many slaves to be free and so it was my turn to live in a free country.

'You helped to make us free.'

'We all helped.'

I take off the garlands to make room for more. I collect the flowers at my feet into a neat pile. The young people return bearing a chair. They coax me into it. I give them a flat refusal. 'An old woman like me can't take too much excitement,' I say. They beg. I tell them if they drop me that would be it, one old woman's death on their hands. They beg some more. To shut them up I comply. They hold me aloft. Not just me but my head still leaning against the door frame and so the house too. The chair has arms and a cushion. The mahogany is polished. They carry me into the crowded square fringed with vendors and in the middle dancers and musicians and spectators making music and dances in response.

Men and women dance and raise a lot of dust. Drums, whistles, horns, singing and clapping fill my ears, nose, eyes and mouth. They dance before me and bow. I clap and laugh and nod. I have seen these figures in other dreams moving like this. I shaped them out of wood. I thought the shapes were trying to rise from the sea, but now I know they were dances. Each figure made by me was in this square. A man, woman or child in some movement to the music. Not movements to the music of the sea, as I had thought. These were dances of freedom. The faces were not scared on those figures but excited. I had made them then read them wrong. Now they were here before me showing me their meaning, and I had helped to shape it. They were dancing not struggling. Ecstatic not terrified. A young woman moves in front of me in a pattern I recognise. I see myself at her age on the deck of the *Zong* in the throes of the fertility dance. She has those movements now bearing down on land, her feet kicking dust into the air, her open palms facing the earth and the sky, drawing one to meet the other. I know what she will do before she does it. I remember. I told it in wood. Now it is here being demonstrated in front of me in sweat, flesh, blood, breath and on land. Earth under sky. Sky invited down to earth. Earth rising to meet sky.

The first thing I did on my arrival in Jamaica as a free woman was buy land. Always my papers would be scrutinised by some incredulous clerk unable to believe that a woman of my standing was free and that she had come all this way to acquire property and live without the protection of a man. I remembered my arrival as a slave when I was counted ashore, no questions asked, and how I fell to the ground and clawed it and kissed it and had to be prised to my feet. My land had to be cleared of tangleweed, stones, brush, shrubs and levelled. Free labour for hire was hard to find, but I refused to pay a slave owner for the use of his slaves. After I built a hut, I planted. A coconut grove. One tree for each soul lost on the *Zong*. Instead of growing vegetables and fruit I planted varieties of trees for their wood. If they bore fruit, all well and good. Children could come and eat them. But I wanted land and wood all around. My proximity to land and wood makes the sea tolerable, almost beautiful; the sea that was spoiled for me. Children in the waves of that sea and the sea playing with them, rolling them in the sand. But I can have nothing to do with it. It is ruined for me. Land and wood protect me from it. Wind in the trees, sometimes rain, obliterate the noise of the sea on the sand. That suits me. To see it from a distance and not be able to hear it breaking on the beach. To watch the children run to and from it and not hear their cries. To see the morning minted in silver coins on the sea and not see its beauty. A poisonous sea. The children drawing the sting from the sea little by little for me. I can look at it. Before I could not. I can't bear to hear it, but sometimes the wind brings it to my open front door and I shudder as if a ghost has crossed the threshold, and I don't slam the door against the ghost, I leave it open, afraid and inquisitive at the same time, inviting that ghost in, since it has made it this far it may as well come in without my say-so, my inquisitiveness feeding it even as I wish for the wind to change direction and take it away, for a breeze to shake that coconut grove and drown out the sea.

A child's voice, a girl's, addresses me. I don't see the child because she is standing in front of the sun and a blinding light shoots at me from all around her head and body. Instead of bothering about that I just incline my head to hear what her voice has to tell me that makes it say my name as if my house is on fire.

'Miss Mintah, there is a white man saying you kept a book that was famous in England.' The girl who tells me this is pointing to the other side of the square. My eyes fail me in the glare. 'What book? What white man? I don't know any white men.'

'He says he is your friend.' Everyone in my vicinity is interested. They listen and look in the direction where the girl points.

'I have no white men as friends.'

'He says he knows you very well.' The young people around me whistle and laugh.

'Do not tease an old woman. It is rude.'

I follow her hand but it leads into a crowd and dust and music. More petals are thrown at me. Rice too. I am garlanded in flowers. *Wake up, Mintah!* There is a man with long white hair talking to a group. He looks familiar. He is white though his skin is tanned brown. I hear him before I recognise him. The group sees me approach and they cheer. Others gather around. The old man holds up a book. His face is lined. His hair is thin on top but long at the sides and white. I don't know those features. But when he smiles I see it is Simon. My ears fill with the sea, brought to me by a breeze I don't feel. My eyes flood with salt water. I hold out my hands to touch some rare wood before me, to feel the run of its grain. My chair is put to the ground and he hugs me up to my feet with the book pressed between me and him. My head swims with the cheering and clapping and whistles.

'Mintah, all my life I search for you.'

'All of mine I been waiting for you.'

Simon and my book are in my arms.

Chapter Thirteen

S HE AWOKE FROM dozing by her front door. Shade had succeeded sun. Simon had not come. The celebration in the breeze swept the square and finished in the trees surrounding her house. There were no garlands or flowers at her feet. Her dream had made her the centre of a parade she was too old to do anything about other than watch. Her life of working with wood was hers alone. Some splinters had been buried so deep in her hand, the skin had hardened over them and now they were forgotten. No one knew her story, because she had not bothered to tell it. All her notes were for herself, her failing memory, her recurrent dreams. These used to hurt her once, like a new splinter, but now she did not know they were there. Time had hardened over them.

Ghosts needed to be fed. She carved and wrote to assuage their hunger. Her life of feeding the ghosts had slowed to the Sunday school, the occasional howdy from the parents of a child she taught and the odd errand run for her by one of the children – money and list of provisions tied in a handkerchief for the child to keep safe. Her dream of Simon was different because this day was new. A parade. Freedom. She was glad he had been a part of her day even if it was a daydream. She lifted the loose left strap over her shoulder and smoothed her dress. With the sun gone her ache would return to her thoughts and shadow every gesture.

This dream was much like the others. People could take what she had to say. Children were seated and they listened without crying or running away. Adults did not doubt that the events had taken place; what they marvelled at was that she had survived such an ordeal. What she had to keep to herself, except to tell it in wood, could at least be lived in her dream-life. More real than being awake. Her dreams were a harbour for her past. It used her body as such. For sustenance. For the life it could not otherwise live since it could not be told.

Now her body was tired, having made all it had seen as she slept. Earth had yielded every secret to her. Now earth too was a body with no more to give. Her hands wanted emptiness for the first time. Wood had shown her everything. Her life had been filled with its peregrinations. She too was tired. Not moving eased those aches. Not breathing too hard. Not breathing for a moment seemed to empty her hands, her head, her heart. The sea sounded in the shell of her ear. Perhaps not the sea but lips held so close to her ear they brushed it as they uttered some secret. She was sure she had dreamed all there was to dream and given shape to them in wood. Yet she inclined her head and stopped breathing so as to catch every word and convert those brushings to kisses. She wanted to be kissed. A slight smile tightened her lips. Somehow smiling made listening that much easier. And not breathing eased the pain, emptied her hands, lightened her head and heart.

She tried to picture land before the *Zong*, before the mission on the coast. There was her father and her mother, the woman she would become. Her father's hands, her mother's head and body. His hand guiding hers, her mother's footsteps ahead of hers. Two loves in another land. A big sea in between. Years of that sea widening in between. A road she could not find now even if she desired it. She was no longer the Mintah who had left that land, those two people. The *Zong* saw to that. The sea had erased whole tracts of the land and the people she had held inside. Wood and her dreams had recovered much to her but not enough to feed her desire to return. Salt had helped with the obliteration of her past. Mintah was buried in trees, in sand. Like a spirit or ghost she had fled into wood and soil. With her father's hands she had sought to redeem herself to herself. His hands and her mother's head and body. Besides which there was no Mintah. The *Zong* and the sea had seen to that. Her hands had been busy; now they wanted to be idle, now that she understood wood, and the sea no longer haunted her. Children played in the sea disarming it of its past. Salt surrendered on the leaves and children licked the salt off those leaves. The air she breathed was washed clean of the sea and salt by those children's tongues. The past with all its salt and water balanced, as she stopped breathing, against all the wood and land in her life.

She always used a needle to pick splinters out of her hands. When her eyes began to fail her she induced children with sugar water and coconut cake to take over the needle and fish out those splinters. Sometimes a child invited to inspect her hand for a splinter she was sure was there would find none. Mintah would insist she could feel the thing putting down roots in her flesh. When enough children came and went without producing a splinter she understood that what ached were the bones in her hand. Eased by the sun, worsened by the sea air. The sea was still her enemy. Her hands wanted to be empty because they could not hold a chisel anymore. Her fingers became knarled and knotted like wood. When she stopped working with wood her dreams ceased using her to rehearse her past.

She could not write anymore. At Sunday school she got the children to repeat after her, and when she lost her train of thought one of the older children would remind her of where she had left off. Other things were slipping from her besides the past. The brushing against her ears was the wind, but she heard very little though she listened hard in expectation of her old enemy, the sea. She even ran her tongue over her lips for the tell-tale sign of salt. She was too old to go around licking leaves.

Her hands had hardened into stumps. Soon someone would come along with a chisel to carve the secrets out of her. How easily would they be able to read her grain? How quickly would she empty? Unlike the sea. Incomparable to salt. Heavy as a tree with deep roots. Unmovable. Wind in the leaves. Salt lacing the leaves. The sea in her ear. Earth underfoot. Sap for blood. Grain instead of veins.

If the sea was not her enemy, then what? She considered her piece of land. The trees she'd planted on it. Her one-room house. Inside was dark and cool. The celebrations seeped out of the wood with the quality of a perfume. She walked to the lamp in the corner near the clay oven, picked it up, shook it, felt that it was empty and found the oil for it, all in the dark. She filled the lamp mainly by touch, her fingers at the nozzle, and struck the match to light it. The flame restored her sight with its warm light, then blinded her with its sudden glare. For a moment all the figures ranged about the room, on shelves, in corners, on the table, beside her bed, under chairs and on the walls, were illuminated by the flame and seemed to dance and leap into the air. The flame took root and branched outwards and upwards. Her bones did not ache during that brief spell. Instead her attention shifted from her bones to her skin. She felt her skin tingle. Her body itched all over. Then her skin burned. This must be what it was like to have someone chisel into you for shapes hidden in you. To lose parts of yourself for some deeper, truer self. Her empty hands grabbed at the flames, as shapely as her carved figures, but shifting, like the sea, and insubstantial to her flesh as the air. Heat filled her hands. Heat undressed her. Fire pushed her to her knees. She opened her mouth for air and ate fire. It stung like the time she had drunk the sea. The flames toppled her, laid her flat and covered her. Then they turned their gaze to the dancing, leaping figures stacked around the house and they glided from her body to every corner of the big room, filling it with the music of the sea and air riddled with salt. The flames licked the salt from the air and then the air itself until the walls of Mintah's house were sucked into the flames, buckled and folded in. Burning wood perfumed Mintah's body and a smell of newly turned earth. Fire danced around her body. Shadows cast by it pranced along the land and leapt above the trees. All her dreamed, unearthed secrets flew back into the ground. The spirits carved in those figures fled into the wooded hills.

Epilogue

W E WERE ALL dead. The ship was full of ghosts. All the cruelties we sustained were maintained by us. Made over hundreds of years, our behaviour could never cease to exist. We needed each other. Our contrast. Opposing views of the sea. Our different fix on the stars. The sea was more than willing to accommodate us. Accustomed to rehearsal, to repeats and returns, it did not care about the abomination happening in its name. We could not stop even if we tried. That ship was in that sea and we were in it and that would be for an eternity in a voyage without beginning or end. That was how I came to the *Zong* and my place on it. I did not find the *Zong*, the *Zong* found me. I have a list of names. I know who did what to whom. But my detailed knowledge has not made an iota of difference to history or to the sea. All the knowledge has done is burden me.

I am in your community, in a cottage or apartment or cardboard box, tucked away in a quiet corner, ruminating over these very things. The *Zong* is on the high seas. Men, women and children are thrown overboard by the captain and his crew. One of them is me. One of them is you. One of them is doing the throwing, the other is being thrown. I'm not sure who is who, you or I. There is no fear, nor shame in this piece of information. There is only the fact of the *Zong* and its unending voyage and those deaths that cannot be undone. Where death has begun but remains unfinished because it recurs. Where there is only the record of the sea. Those spirits are fled into wood. The ghosts feed on the story of themselves. The past is laid to rest when it is told.